WELCOME TO THE FAMILY

BLOOD IN, BLOOD OUT

ALEX J. FISCHER

For my Family and Friends

1

———

Roger walked down the long hallway and came to a stop in front of a wooden podium with a ripped man in a formal suit behind it. "Wait over there, Mr. Johnson," the man in a tie said pointing to Roger's right at some seats along the wall. He stood in front of a large double door with his hand out. "The boss is busy at the moment."

Roger walked over the plush red carpet to a row of chairs pushed against the wall and took a seat. "No worries." He leaned back and kicked his feet out. He felt a rumble in his pants pocket and pulled out his phone. "Oh, great," he said under his breath. He pushed the screen and brought it to his ear. "Hello?"

An immature, high pitched voice answered back. "Bub? Is that you?"

"That's right. What's wrong, Sis?"

"Mom and Dad are arguing again. I think that one guy called. They're really loud this time."

"I'll be back as soon as I can. Okay? I have to meet my boss, and then I'll be right home."

He heard a sniffle on the other end. "You promise?"

"Of course," Roger said. "Just stay in your room, and don't interrupt them. Alright? If you hear footsteps going up the stairs, hop in bed and pretend you're asleep if you have to."

"I got it. Please hurry."

"I'll go as fast as I can. Be strong. I'm on my way." He pressed the screen and shoved the device down his pants pocket. He looked up to see the glasses wearing guard staring at him. "You don't want to know."

The guard shrugged his shoulders and resumed his scanning the hallway without a word.

The sound of a door opening caused both men to snap their attention further down the hallway. A half-naked, sturdy man wearing only underwear appeared. He slammed it shut and talked loud enough to be heard. "You're nuts. I said no. I'm out of here, you crazy broad. We're done." He took off into a dead sprint toward them.

Just stay out of it. You want nothing to do with this circus, Roger thought. He looked down at his shoes, only to see a pair of bare feet stop in front of him.

He raised a hand in front of his face as his eyes traced their way upward. "Aw, come on, man." He craned his neck up to see the man's bushy mustached face. "Yes? Can I help you?"

"Hey, new guy, give me your dress pants."

"I'm sorry, what? Are you serious, sir?"

A new, different, altogether feminine voice echoed through the hall along with another slam. "Get back here, Bruce!"

"Damn it," Bruce said. Without warning he jogged off and disappeared through the nearest door.

Roger looked back where he had come from to see a

buxom young woman exiting the room and giving chase. *Is that the boss's daughter? Oh boy.*

She came to a stop in front of the guard. "You there. Did you see where he went?"

"I'm sorry, Ms. Morris. No, I didn't."

She pursed her ruby red lips together. "You're useless." She crossed her arms under her considerable chest. She huffed, causing her shoulder length black hair to bounce. She glanced over at Roger. "What are you looking at?"

He looked away from her back to the door and guard. "Nothing."

"Good. Keep it that way. It's creepy."

Roger got to his feet and stood face to face. "Excuse me?"

She got in his face. Her breath tickled his nose as she spoke. "What are you, deaf or just stupid? Do you have any idea who I am?"

Roger saw the guard over her shoulder shaking his head and drawing his hand across his throat. He looked back at her cerulean eyes. "I have a pretty good idea."

"Then know your place, and get out of my sight."

Roger grinned. "I can't do that, or your father would have my head. Sorry about that. Really, I am."

She took a step backward, threw her head back, and muttered under her breath. "Asshole."

Loud stomping came from the nearby door. The guard opened it, revealing an immaculately dressed older man with armed guards on either side. His thinning gray hair clung to his widow's peak as he stopped in front of them. "What's all this noise out here? Ah, Mr. Johnson. Please come in. I'm sorry about my daughter." He rubbed his bulbous nose with his thumb before continuing. "She can be a bit loud. She wasn't any trouble, was she?"

"No, sir. Not at all."

"Good." He beckoned Roger over, threw an arm around his shoulder, and guided him toward the now open room. "Lizzy, give us some privacy. Would you, princess?"

"Yeah, sure," she huffed. "I'll leave you two alone." She stomped off back toward her room and disappeared inside.

"Come on inside, Mr. Johnson. I'm Bernard, but we prefer to keep it formal when conducting business. I'm sorry to have kept you waiting. You know how business can be. Right, son?" He turned and led him inside, leaving the two men behind watching Roger as they passed them.

"Of course, sir."

The guards closed the door behind them and remained stationed just inside.

Roger scanned the inside of the room to see far more people than he initially guessed. Rows of men lined the sides of the carpet leading up to the large, imposing desk. Two men stood on either side of the seat behind the desk. Behind them were large windows with trees visible outside. Bernard left his side, moved around the ornate desk, sat down, and motioned to the seat in front of it. "You've made quite the splash. You're quite the earner I hear. You've helped our resident techie on quite a number of profitable online ventures in the last ten years, according to her."

Roger sat and looked down at the desk. "I do everything in my power, sir." Roger kept his gaze on the desk in front of him.

"That's what I like to hear. Mr. Johnson, look at me please."

Roger raised his head and locked his brown eyes with the older man.

"Good man. You've had quite a few of my boys vouch for you." His lips smacked with a pause. "Do you understand what that means?"

A bead of sweat trickled down the side of his head. He answered with a shake of his head.

"It means you've been selected to join the family proper." He looked to his right and nodded. "Daniel my boy, now if you please."

The black haired man to Bernard's right placed a revolver and a knife on the table in front of him. He leaned forward, placing his palms on the surface, and glared at Roger. His chestnut eyes pierced through him as he spoke. "You will carry out the family's business with these. Give me your hand."

Roger extended his hand toward the young man's until it was grasped. He turned Roger's hand palm side up and grabbed the knife in his other hand. He pricked Roger's ring finger and squeezed until blood oozed out.

Bernard placed a cigar into the corner of his mouth. "With this, you're nearly one of us now. You only have one thing left to do." He looked at the man beside Roger. "Daniel, my son, do you want to explain?"

Daniel placed the knife back on the desk and towered over Roger, causing his jet-black hair to shift, obscuring his pointed glare. "It'd be my pleasure, Dad." He again slammed his palms on the desk in front of him. "We have a problem, kid, and you're going to be the one to fix it for us. There's just one thing you have to do first."

Roger pocketed the weapons in front of him. "Yes?"

"You're going to take the oath we all did. You listen to me and memorize this, then repeat it. 'I will put the Morris family first above all else. I will destroy our enemies and support my brothers no matter the cost.'"

"I will put the Morris family first above all else, I will destroy our enemies and support my brothers no matter the cost."

Daniel turned back to his father. "I think he's ready."

"Then begin showing me you're a leader, Son. He's your responsibility now."

Daniel had a wide smile as he turned back to Roger. He reached down, grabbed his wrist, yanked him up into a standing position, and released his hand. "Come with me and finish your rebirth, kid." He led him back toward the door, past the lines of men. "Don't worry, gentlemen. We'll be right back to celebrate."

Daniel passed through the doorway and talked without turning around. "Close the door."

Roger did so as he exited and continued following Daniel until he led him to the stairs leading down. "Is it out of place to ask what exactly I'm doing?"

"Yes, actually it is," Daniel said. "Lucky for you, I'm not a huge stickler for rules. Are you familiar with the term 'blood in, blood out'?"

"Yes."

"Well, someone tried to leave early without my father's go ahead. He tried to defect to a local group called the Ninth Street Enforcers. They're our direct competitors. Is that enough explanation?"

"Yes, Mr. Morris."

"Don't call me that. I'm not old yet. Call me sir if you must." They reached the bottom of the stairs and exited the nearby door to come to a large backyard. A suffocating tree line encircled the yard and the sides of the house. A solitary light mounted above the door illuminated a lone man lying next to a hole and a pile of dirt with a shovel wedged inside it. He wriggled back and forth and jerked around on the grass. His hands were behind him, bound together along with his feet with a zip tie.

"You're not escaping those zip ties, Marvin. I tied them

myself," Daniel said with a laugh. He walked up beside the hole and turned to face Roger. He pulled out his own firearm from the front of his pants. He leveled it at Roger. "Go on, kid. Use that new piece and take care of him for us."

Roger raised his hands in the air.

Daniel lowered his hands. "What are you doing?"

"Don't shoot me please, sir."

Daniel brought a hand up to his forehead and sighed. "Oh, for God's sake. I won't. It's just a safety precaution, kid. Hurry up already. The boys are waiting to welcome you." He brought his nine-millimeter up again.

Roger reached into his jacket with shaking hands and removed the revolver. He walked over to the tied-up man and pointed the end at his head. His arm shook.

"What's the hold up?" Daniel asked. "Squeeze the trigger already. Prove you can take care of yourself and your brothers in arms."

"I can't just kill an unarmed man like this. Can I?"

Daniel pulled back the hammer with a click. "That's too bad. Here's the way this is going to work. There are two options here. Option one is you kill him and kick him in that damned hole. We both go upstairs and laugh this off. Option two is I kill the both of you and I go back up there alone. What's it going to be?"

"That's a pretty shitty choice, sir."

"Welcome to life. You have ten seconds to decide before I do."

Roger looked down at the man. Incoherent moans escaped his duct taped mouth. "I'm truly sorry about this." He closed his eyes and squeezed the trigger. His arm flew up. A flash of light and a thunderous crack broke the silence.

Roger stood there, arm still extended, looking down at

the man. He heard crunching grass coming closer. "I just killed a man," he whispered with a shaking voice.

He felt an arm fling around his shoulders and pull him close. "Damned right you did," Daniel laughed. "Put that away now, brother. He's dead. Let's send him on his way, yeah?" He placed his foot on Marvin's shoulder.

Roger nodded, absentmindedly holstered his weapon, and placed his foot beside Daniel's. He pushed and the body flopped into the grave. He looked up at the now smiling man. "We're just going to leave him here at the boss's place? Shouldn't we like dump the body somewhere and burn it or something?"

Daniel's head leaned back in a laugh. "That's a good point, but don't worry. We have a team on the way here as we speak. This was all just a song and dance for your benefit. They'll take this shitbag and dump him where no one will ever find him. That's good looking out though. It shows you know what you're doing. Besides, no one will have heard that gunshot. We're too far out into the countryside. Why do you think we settled out here? Now let's go already." They walked side by side back toward the building. "Let's go and celebrate." They climbed the stairs to the inside.

"No offense, sir, but I need to get back to my home," Roger said, pushing the back door open. "My family is going through a bit of a-"

They winded their way back upstairs and Daniel removed his arm from Roger's shoulders. "We'll deal with that right after father formalizes your joining. That's not negotiable, buddy."

"I get it."

"A good man never complains when adversity rears its ugly head. You're making this teaching you the rules thing easy, kid." Daniel motioned toward the guard outside his father's office. "We've got a freshly popped cherry boy here."

The man chuckled and pushed open the door with a quiet, "Welcome to the family."

Daniel pushed him forward between the lines of men.

Roger stepped forward. The men gave a small bow as he passed. He came to a stop in front of the desk before Bernard.

The old man stood up and circled around the desk. He enveloped him in a hug before taking a step backward. "Welcome to the Morris family. Remember the lessons of loyalty you learned today, son. Now go and meet your brothers. If you'll excuse me, gentlemen, I have an important appointment to keep tonight." One of the men at his side helped him put on his coat. They navigated their way past Roger and, without further word, left.

The door slammed shut and a cacophony of voices bombarded his ears. He turned and saw a few familiar faces stepping up to him. A crowd of people on the other side of the room kept to themselves.

"Mr. Johnson," Bruce greeted. "I guess you're not as much of a pussy as the odds said you were."

A man with greased back hair at his side elbowed Bruce in his ribs. "Don't listen to this simpleton. We're glad to have you, Roger. I'm Eddy. If you ever need anything or have any questions, you ask me. Alright? I'll get you anything you want: weapons, body armor, grenades, and any kind of tech you could want." The toothpick between his lips danced left and right.

"For the right price," Daniel said from behind Roger.

"That goes without saying. Right?" Eddy asked. "You can't pay, you don't play."

Roger nodded. "I'll remember that. Thanks."

A smoky feminine voice interrupted their conversation. "Is that the new guy?"

The men stepped aside and looked behind them. Elizabeth walked forward and stopped in front of the group. "Oh, it's him."

Roger's voice fell quiet. "Oh Lord."

"Liz," Daniel called with an outstretched hand. "I didn't know you'd be here to welcome our newest brother."

"Who? Oh, that guy. No, I'm not here for him." She moved toward Bruce and placed a hand on his shoulder. Her voice was coated in sugar. "I'm here for this sad sack. We never got to finish our talk earlier, did we?" Her hand gripped down.

Bruce's eyes darted through the group until they stopped on Roger. He slipped out from under her grasp and moved to his side. He threw his arm around his neck and pulled him closer. "I'm sorry, honey, but I need to help out the new guy tonight."

Roger's eyebrows shot up as he looked at the man beside him.

"He's not lying," Daniel said. "We're going to go help the new guy take care of a little family problem."

"Hell, if you boys are going, I am too." Eddy poked a thumb into his chest. "Without me, what are you losers going to do? Besides, it has to be more fun than standing around here." He moved to the free side of Roger. "What do you say, kid? Let's go fix that problem of yours."

"It's settled." Daniel clapped. "Who's driving?"

"I will." Bruce moved away from Roger and placed a hand over his stomach. "The last time you drove I got sick."

On the road...

"How much are your folks into this guy for?" Eddy asked from Roger's side in the back seat.

Roger looked past Eddy out the window at the passing buildings. "Since my sister is sick, tens of thousands. He's also threatened us before. He claimed he'd take her and sell her off to pay the debt. He said he'd have us killed if we resisted. I've held him off with everything I've had, but it's been getting worse lately. He's getting more aggressive."

"How old is your sister?

"She's six," Roger said. He pulled out his wallet and retrieved a picture of him and his brunette sister together smiling, cheek to cheek. "Here's a picture of her." He handed the picture to Eddy.

"Mother of Christ." Eddy's hand traced the cross across his chest. "This guy we're dealing with is a real piece of work. I can't believe anyone with a God given soul would even think of tainting such a girl."

"The last time I confronted him wasn't exactly pretty either. I think I pissed him off when I broke his nose."

Eddy laughed out loud and looked to the front. "Danny, did you hear that?"

Daniel cracked his knuckles. "Yeah. He sounds like a real piece of shit." He looked up into the rearview mirror. "Don't worry. When we're done, he'll never even contact your family again if he knows what's good for him."

"Thanks, boys," Roger said.

"Don't even mention it. It's our pleasure, Rook," Eddy said.

"If the fucker's using a small girl as leverage, I want to give the guy a piece of my mind," Bruce said, keeping his eyes on the road. The car turned onto a deserted road. Rows of cars lined the sides of the street with a lone building ahead. The pavement was cracked and grimy. Windswept litter passed by on the empty sidewalk outside. Bruce slowed down and put the van in park. "We're here. His place is up about a block on the left."

"Let's go teach him some manners," Daniel said as he opened the door. Everyone followed suit and walked shoulder to shoulder down the street. They saw a lone single floor building at the end of the road. Its windows could barely be seen through, the bricks on the outside were stained with unspeakable filth.

They reached the door of the poorly kept building, and Roger led them inside. He held the door open behind him as he called out. "Mr. Thomas, I'm here to make another payment." He scanned the inside of the office. Rows of people were lined up in front of numerous chalkboards. A television above showed horses racing forward.

Two tall, well-built young men came out of a door in the back of the smoky establishment. They marched up to the group and stopped a few feet away. "What are you doing here?" The taller, more muscular man asked. "Did we not make it obvious you weren't welcome last time?" He reached forward and grabbed Roger's collar, pulling him forward. "Leave before things get ugly again, Mr. Johnson," he growled.

Eddy spoke from Roger's right. "Remove that hand right now before you lose it."

The man looked toward Eddy. "Fuck you. Who are you? This isn't your business, slick. This deadbeat and his family are behind on their debt."

Eddy chuckled and looked at the men beside him. His right hand snaked around his back. "Fuck me?" He turned to the crowd and raised his voice. It was firm, but undeniably polite sounding. "Did you hear that, ladies and gentlemen? Now would probably be a good time to leave, unless you suffer from spontaneous blindness and memory loss." His voice lost its courteous tone and took on an undeniable edge as he finished. "Do you understand me?"

Hushed whispers and hurried footsteps were the only sound, along with the creaking of the door.

Daniel and Bruce circled around the two men in the now abandoned room and stood a few feet away. "They always choose the hard way." Daniel dashed forward and placed the quiet bouncer into a full nelson while Bruce simply grabbed the larger man's hand behind his back and twisted the thumb, eliciting a groan.

Eddy lunged forward and clutched the remaining arm holding Roger. His right hand launched forward with a flash. His knife plunged into the forearm until it was handle deep. A sickening squelch echoed across the now silent room, along with a howl of pain.

The hand released its grip on Roger as the man stumbled back into Bruce.

"Fuck me?" Eddy asked. "Fuck you." He kicked the front of the man's leg, causing him to stumble to a knee. He threw a left hook, causing the man to tumble to the floor.

"I almost forgot my knife." Eddy knelt and grasped the handle. "Sorry, mate. I just need this back." He yanked the blade free, causing a river of blood to begin flowing onto the wood below. He flicked the blade down at the floor, spattering the hardwood below with crimson fluid. "Where's the boss man anyway?"

The quiet, bug eyed man in Daniel's grasp pointed at a door behind the counter.

Eddy walked up to him and sheathed his knife. "That's a smart man. If only most people were as cooperative as you."

"As a reward, you can take a little nap." Daniel shifted his arms to the man's neck and squeezed. His victim's hands reached up and started clawing at Daniel's arms wrapped around his neck. His face turned blue eventually. After a few minutes the bouncer's eyes rolled up in the back of his head and he collapsed. "Rog, you and Eddy go get our guest of honor, would you? I'll explain to this conscious one what'll happen if anyone calls the police on this afterward. That's assuming he can quit crying like a bitch. Look at him writhing on the ground. I'll make him listen."

"It'd be our pleasure," Eddy said with a wide smile. "Come on, Rog. Let's go let him know your debt's been cleared."

Bruce delivered a withering kick to the unconscious man's head below. "While you're doing that, I'm going to go and delete the surveillance footage." He moved just behind the counter toward the stack of electronic devices. He pushed a button, and a video cassette popped out. He pocketed it and moved back.

Roger rubbed his hand and looked down at the squirming, bleeding man below. "I'll be right with you." He threw a vicious kick into his ribs before moving toward Eddy. He led him back behind the counters to a door in the corner of the room labeled 'Manager's Office'. He tried the door, only to find it wouldn't budge. He pounded on the door. "Thomas? I'm here with a payment."

A low, almost imperceptible click came from within the room. Roger pushed Eddy, causing him to tumble to the side of the door. He ended up beside him on the floor.

As soon as the two men hit the ground, a thunderous swarm of bullets shattered the quiet. The door groaned and creaked open after the assault had ended. A voice from inside called out, "Just stay away. I have more where that came from."

Roger removed his hands from his ears and looked at Eddy beside him on the ground. "You alright, man?"

Eddy gave a gentle slap to Roger's cheek. "Yeah, kid. Thanks. I owe you one." The two men stood back up and stayed to the side of the door.

Daniel's booming voice came from the main room. "Hurry up, boys. We have to get out now. The cops are no doubt on their way after that noise."

Eddy pulled a pistol out of his dress coat and angled it around the corner. He squeezed the trigger and was rewarded with a blood curdling scream. "There, now we're even. The Johnson family debt is settled and null. You hear me? He's with the Morris family now. If you so much as call them, I swear to God himself I'll come back here and won't stop until you have a new venting hole in your head. He bent down and picked up the expended cartridges. He slapped the back of Roger's shoulder. "Now let's get out of here, brother."

2
_____

Roger sighed and twisted the key, causing the engine to shut off. He rubbed his eyes, then looked at the clock by his radio. "Two a.m. already? It'd sure be nice if they were asleep. What are the odds of that?" he asked himself. His voice fell to a whisper. "No chance in hell." He pulled out his wallet. "Better safe than sorry." He extracted four one hundred-dollar bills and shoved them into his back pocket.

He opened the door and stepped out. As he approached the front door of the two-story house, he reached into his coat pocket and retrieved a key. He unlocked the door and stepped inside the silent house.

"No lights. Maybe they're asleep," he whispered and stalked through the pitch black to the nearby stairs leading up.

"Where were you at, boy?" His father's gruff voice called out from behind as the lights snapped on.

Roger squinted and raised a hand above his eyes as he turned around at the foot of the stairs. "Out."

"Do you have any idea what time it is? Your mother

worried herself sick because of you." He eyed his son up and down. "Though with that getup I can guess. You were out earning from that Morris family again. Weren't you?"

Roger looked toward his shoes and shuffled his feet.

"I thought so." His father took a step forward. "Do you remember what I told you about those crooks? Don't get mixed up with them. You're better than that. You're a better man than them." He flicked Roger's dress coat. "They may be all dressed up, rich, and suave, but you know what they'll eventually get?"

The two spoke at the same time. "A trip to the hospital if they're lucky, or the morgue."

His father took a calmer tone. "Look, Son, I appreciate the help. But I don't want you anywhere near those people. I've heard stories about them. They've been known to shake down shops, blackmail, and even shoot people. Let me and your mother worry about the finances. You just worry about getting a normal job. Okay?"

Roger stared off over his dad's shoulder. "Yeah, Dad," he said in a weary voice.

Rushing footsteps from upstairs soon approached. A loud female voice interrupted them. "Keith, is he back?"

"Yeah, Beatrice. He's home."

A tall female form flew down the stairs and completely enveloped Roger in a bear hug.

"There you are. Where were you? I was so worried." She released him and backed up a step.

His father cleared his throat and moved to his mother's side. He placed an arm around her waist. "He was out with his friends partying, honey. Don't worry. He just forgot to call. Isn't that right, Son?"

The corners of Roger's mouth inched upward. "Sorry about that."

His mother leaned her head on his father's shoulder. "It's okay, pumpkin. Just try not to make it a habit." She released a massive yawn. "Okay, boys, I'm going to bed. Your mother needs her beauty sleep after all. Good night." She climbed the stairs, leaving the two men alone again.

Keith grunted, "Don't make me do that again, Son. I despise lying to your mother."

"Sorry, Dad."

"So, how much did you make tonight?"

"Seriously? A couple hundred."

His father held out a palm. "Give me the privacy tax then. You know the drill. All of it."

Roger fished the wallet out of his back pocket and deposited two one hundred-dollar bills.

"Good. Now go to bed already, you delinquent."

"Good night," Roger said as he climbed the stairs.

Roger trudged up the stairs. He saw that the door to his right was left open, with loud snoring coming from within.

The door beside it was ajar. A small series of coughs drew his attention to it. A pair of jade green eyes stared at him through the crack. A small hand wrapped around the outside of the door. A reserved voice came from the occupant's mouth "Bub, you're finally home?" His sister fully opened the door and stood there in her blue pajamas.

"That's right." He squatted down and rubbed the top of her head. "What are you still doing up, munchkin? Shouldn't you be asleep by now? You're going to be tired for school tomorrow."

"You said you'd be home soon when I called earlier," she looked away, "so I waited up."

Roger sighed, a genuine smile finding its way to his face. He stood up. "Come on then. Let's go get you tucked in."

Her face lit up and she disappeared behind the wooden door.

He entered the small room. It was pitch black, other than the moonlight pouring in from the window across from him. A toy chest lay under the window with stuffed animals of all kinds stacked on top. A small television sat to its left. A twin bed, directly to his left, lined the wall, along with a small table with a device perched on top. Untold wires connected to a small mask and coat sat on top of it.

He sat on the bed, reaching over to the nightstand and grabbing the mask. "Come on. I know you don't like it, but you have to, Michelle."

"I hate it. It makes it hard to sleep," she wheezed.

"This is not a debate. You need to be able to breathe. Dad may forget, but I won't." He placed the mask over her mouth and nose and pushed a button on the device. It whirred to life. "Lift them up."

Michelle lifted her arms above her head as he slid the coat over her.

"There, now you should be able to cough that gunk up."

He stood up and made his way to the chest. He plucked a Koala bear from the pile and brought it back to the bed. "We don't want to forget this, do we?"

She hugged the bear to her chest and slipped her feet under the covers.

He raised the blankets up over her shoulders. "There we go. Now, time for you to sleep already."

Her hand reached up and grabbed his as he prepared to turn away. "Thanks, Bubbie."

He reached a hand out and placed it on her shoulder. "You just worry about any tests you have tomorrow. Okay? Let me worry about everything else."

"Mmhmm." She nuzzled into the puffy pillow.

He left her room and moved to his at the end of the hardwood hallway. He shut the door behind him and locked it. Leaning back, he slid down to the ground. He shook his head as he brought both hands up to his forehead. Tears slipped out of the corners of his eyes. He whispered into his hands with a cracking voice. "I killed a man today. What have I done?"

3

"It looks like you'll be getting your first job, Rog," Daniel said. He looked down at the paper in his hands. "You'll be coming with us tonight to guard the boss. The only problem is that we need a guy good with tech before we go. Are you any good with," he paused and drug his finger across a line, "'configuring listening devices remotely?"

"I've set one by hand before in training, but not remotely."

Daniel clicked his tongue. "Then it looks like you're due for a little refresher course. You've been to the tech department before, right?"

"It's where I was first put when I was just an associate, yes. I learned a lot there."

Daniel crumpled the paper and tossed it over his shoulder onto the carpet below. "It looks like you'll have a homecoming then, doesn't it? Don't get too comfortable in the egghead lair. We leave at eight tonight. Report outside at least five minutes before, and come strapped. Am I understood?"

"Yes, sir."

"Good. Now go and learn. I'm going to the range while you're doing that. Later." Daniel turned and exited via the nearest door.

Roger went out the other door in the room and made his way through the winding passageways. He soon came to a door labeled with a lone word, 'Computers'. He knocked twice. Receiving no answer, he twisted the knob and pushed. The door collided with something and stopped. A squeak, along with a variety of curse words, serenaded his ears. "Just a second. Okay, come in."

Roger entered and saw a short, blonde haired girl sitting in front of a desktop with multiple monitors. Wires ran all over the floor. A stack of papers sat on the desk beside her. "Sorry to interrupt, Tanya, but I was sent here."

"That voice?" she asked, not bothering to turn to face him. "Give me just a second." Her hands danced across the keyboard. She spun her chair around. "You join at eighteen, work down here ten years, then get promoted. I'll be honest, I never expected to see you again." She got to her feet, came over, and gave him a gentle hug "How's your sister doing?"

"She's better. Thanks. She absolutely adored the last time when you talked to her over webcam. I need to get that software you used to disguise your cam footage as a fox. She wouldn't stop talking about it."

She stepped back. "That reminds me. Did you hear about the new medication that came out for Pulmonary Fibrosis? It's supposed to give ten percent more lung function. I just read about it today. The only problem is it costs nearly six figures for a year's treatment.

Roger pulled out his pants pockets. "I can't really afford that at the moment. Which brings me to why I'm here."

"I assume you're here to learn how to use this?" She held up a tiny dot in her palm.

"That's right. I've no idea why I am, but the boss's son said to."

She scoffed. "That oaf? Tell me you're not working with him."

"He's my boss now."

"Then that means I have to teach you every little thing. That moron can't manage to log in to a pc, much less calibrate a sensitive listening device." She gestured to a nearby empty desk. "Let's get started."

He followed her with caution, picking his feet up over wires strewn across the floor. "You certainly have strong opinions on Mr. Morris."

"Let's just say I've dealt with him before." She shivered. "He's arrogant, rude, and a brute. He always thinks he's right.

"I think that's in the job description of a wise guy."

Her voice fell to a mere whisper. "Then who knows how you got pulled up." She rolled up her sleeves, revealing her lithe arms. "Let's get to work already. The sooner we're done, the sooner I can get back to the new open source project I'm working on. We don't have all day."

"We do actually," Roger said. "It's nine a.m., and I have to leave by seven thirty p.m. at the latest"

She gave a punch to his shoulder. "Just pay attention, Rog."

"Okay."

That night...

Roger shoved his hands into his pants pockets. Rain pelted the concrete below him. He pulled out his phone and checked the time. "I'm not late," he said to himself. He gazed back at the front door of the complex. "This is the place. Right?"

The front door opened, revealing a large procession. Daniel, Eddy, Bruce, Elizabeth, and finally Bernard made their way outside.

"You're early. Good," Daniel said as he approached. "Let's get saddled up and go before we all catch colds."

Bernard and Elizabeth climbed into the backseat of the nearby van first. Daniel sat in the front driver's seat.

Roger flung both rear doors open, stepped aside letting everyone else go first, climbed in last, and sat down on the side of the cabin. He reached over and slammed both doors shut.

He could hear Daniel from the front seat. "We're good. Let's go."

Roger felt an elbow dig into his side. He turned and saw Bruce polishing his weapon with a handkerchief. "What are you packing, newbie?"

"Something bigger than a .22." He reached inside his coat and produced two revolvers.

"Is that a .357? I wouldn't think someone with noodle arms would want that much of a donkey kick. Are you even ambidextrous?" He chuckled. "Oh, I get it. When one empties, you just switch so you don't waste time reloading. Am I right?"

Roger noticed a tuft of black hair and a pair of cerulean eyes peaking over the seat at them. "That would work. I prefer to just launch as much high caliber lead downrange as soon as I can."

Eddy leaned forward and inspected them. "Let's just hope you can hit what you're aiming at. That's a short barrel, and double action has the nasty habit of impeding accuracy in my experience." He leaned back and kicked his foot out. "Still, those are damned nice."

"We won't be needing them," Bernard barked from over the seat. "This is a sit down we're going to, not a battlefield. Is everything ready, boy?"

"Yes, sir," Roger said. He placed a magnum onto his lap and reached into his pants pocket. He retrieved a tiny black dot sitting in the middle of his palm. He looked up to see a solitary hand reaching up over the backseat. Elizabeth's eyes narrowed.

Roger reached across Bruce and extended his palm. "Just get it near him. It'll get everything."

"Give it to me already." She snatched it and disappeared behind the seat.

Roger stuck his weapons back inside the holsters in his coat and looked at Eddy. He leaned forward, whispering. "Who are we meeting anyway?"

"The soon to be mayor of New York. I hear the guy's a prick. Still, having the mayor in our pocket should open some doors. Right?"

Bruce stuck his weapons down the back of his pants. "Yeah. I hear he wants to implement 'safety' laws for firearms. Apparently, a lot of people want to be disarmed."

Roger scratched his head. "Why exactly? Wait a minute, is that even constitutional?"

"Who knows?" Eddy asked. "It just means we'll be one of the only armed outfits around. That's all I care about. God bless 'progress'."

"It's better than that, boys," Bernard said. "Favors are what we're doing this for. Maybe those fucking Enforcers will be the victim of a massive police manhunt while our new mayor takes a tough stance on gun crime."

Daniel laughed. "Yeah, and I bet the mayor could keep

the police off our backs within reason." He looked up at the rear-view mirror. "Eddy, you're with me when we get there. Bruce, you and Rog are on patrol outside. I want you two to stay together in case anyone shows up. Try to handle it quietly first. Alright? No shooting unless absolutely necessary."

"Quite," Bernard said, still looking forward. "These political snot rags aren't fit to be called men. Their knees shake at just getting yelled at. We don't want him getting spooked with a body dropping if we can help it."

"Understood," Bruce said.

Daniel leaned forward and looked out the window to his right. "We're here. Scouts in the back out first and secure the area."

Eddy reached forward and slapped Roger's knee. "That's your cue, kid."

Roger opened the door to his left and hopped out onto the pavement. He surveyed left and right until he was pushed forward by a large hand.

"Move," Bruce said. "We'll check this side first." He pointed over Roger's shoulder down the nearest alley between buildings. He took the lead and moved into the shadows.

Roger jogged to catch up with him and walked just behind him. His jaw dropped as he looked over the decrepit building. "This isn't the first place I'd imagine meeting a politician. Do they normally hang out in the slums in an abandoned office building?"

"Did you think we'd be driving to the guy's upper crust house or something? Think big picture. How would that look if the press got wind that Ronald Alexander met with a bunch of guys like us? It'd tank his mayoral run into the ground."

"I didn't think of that."

"Think before you speak, and it happens less I find."

They turned the corner. Roger cleared his throat. "Fair warning here. I think Miss Morris was giving you the evil eye in the van."

Bruce stopped in his tracks. "What business is that of yours?"

"I did kind of cover for you before. Remember my initiation?"

Bruce growled and brought a hand up to his mustache. "Fair enough. Look, kid, we're not what you'd call together anymore. You probably remember that part." He turned to face Roger and spoke in a firm voice. "Don't get involved with her. She's crazy and doesn't take no for an answer." He walked forward again, causing Roger to jog to catch up.

"She seemed nice enough," Roger said with a wide smile.

Bruce shook his head and turned the corner. "On your head be it. She's cute, sexy, and domineering. If that's what gets you off, go for it. I'm done with her. The question is, when will she be done with me?"

"Judging from that glare earlier, that might be sooner than you think."

"I hope so," Bruce said at his side.

They emerged back onto the street and came up on the side of the van. Bruce knocked on the backseat's passenger window. "It's all clear." They stepped back and everyone filed out.

Daniel led the group inside the building, leaving just Roger and Bruce outside in the rain.

4

Daniel moved to the side of the oaken door and opened it. Eddy and Elizabeth filed in, followed by Bernard. Daniel moved to follow and closed the door behind him. Elizabeth sat on the left side of the table and Daniel on the right.

A conference table dominated the room. Three men awaited them inside. One man sat at the far end of the table with two visibly armed men on either side behind him.

The seated man greeted them in a suave voice. "Ah, Mr. Morris. It's nice to finally make your acquaintance."

Bernard pulled out the opposite seat, took off his coat, and sat down. Eddy stood behind him with crossed arms, glaring at the armed men across the room. "Likewise, Mr. Alexander. Sorry about being late. I had a few things to attend to. You understand."

"Call me Ronald, Mr. Morris. We are friends after all."

"Call me Bernard then, friend." Bernard reached up and removed his bowler hat. He placed it down on the table. "So, let's get down to brass tacks since we both have busy schedules."

Ronald leaned forward. "Quite. I'll make this quick then. I need votes for this next election. As you know, I'm basing my main platform on public safety."

"Via firearm safety regulations, yes. How can we help with that exactly?"

"There is a certain group that opposes this. They claim it's against their fundamental American rights. You know how gun nuts are. They need to be persuaded that it's a good idea for everyone to acquiesce. If violent gun crimes were to say, rise, then it'd bolster public support. Public safety is paramount of course. You get me?"

Bernard looked to his right at Daniel. "The Morris family is a leading proponent of civil reform, Ronald. I think we can get it done. I just want one thing clear."

"If this is about my side, don't worry. You'll be compensated, Bernard. The boys in blue will give your establishments a wide berth. I'll squash any investigations once I'm elected. Fair enough?"

Bernard pointed across the table at him. "Just remember, I collect on debts, Ronald. Don't try to screw us. You won't like it. This isn't some congressional hearing with just a little media backlash. You fuck us, and all the bodyguards in the world won't keep you safe. I say that in the friendliest way possible. You're in politics. You understand, don't you?"

Ronald gulped. He reached up and fiddled with his tie "Yes, I understand, sir. I'm a man of my word."

"For you and your men's sake, I hope you're not lying." Bernard clapped his hands together. "I'm glad we could come to an understanding so easily." He turned to Elizabeth on his left. "I guess politicians can tell the truth sometimes, Sweetie. You were right." He turned back to Ronald with a beaming smile. "Unless there's something else, I believe our business meeting is adjourned, gentlemen."

Everyone at the table stood up. Ronald and his two bodyguards circled around the table.

Daniel and Eddy moved to either side of Bernard. Their eyes narrowed at the approaching group.

Bernard placed his arms out in front of them. "Easy, boys. The good future mayor is just being friendly. Isn't that right?" He reached a hand out to Ronald.

Ronald took it and shook it with a firm squeeze. "That's right, gentlemen. I hope to work together with you for the foreseeable future after all." He extended a hand toward Daniel.

He gripped it and spoke through clenched teeth. "I look forward to it."

Elizabeth bumped her brother away and followed suit. "It should prove to be quite a profitable alliance." She withdrew her hand. "May I give you a piece of advice, Mr. Alexander?"

"Why certainly," he said with a nod.

"Don't waste that campaign money we donated. The voting populace tends to see that as irresponsible. Who'd vote for a wasteful mayor after all?"

Bernard guffawed. "She reminds me more of her mother every day."

"Thank you for the counsel, Ms. Morris. I'll take it to heart," Ronald said.

Eddy helped Bernard into his coat and moved to open the door they had come in.

Bernard grunted and put on his hat. "With that we're off, gentlemen. Be sure to watch the news, sir. It'll give you some ideas for talking points after all. Best of luck in your electoral race, Mr. Alexander." He turned around and exited.

Eddy took point and led them back outside. He opened

the glass double doors and saw Roger to his left. Bruce was leaning against the van.

Bruce scoffed. "You're paranoid, kid. It's just a homeless guy. He's probably looking to get warm is all."

Roger was looking down the sidewalk to his left toward a lone man walking in the rain in their direction. He had a revolver down at his side in one hand ready.

Eddy snapped his fingers. "Let's get ready. The boss is right behind me."

Bruce snapped to attention, moved to the side, and gripped the door handle.

The glass door opened again. This time Bernard, Daniel, and Elizabeth emerged. They reached halfway to the van when Roger's voice pierced the patter of the rain.

"He's got a gun. Get down!" A deafening crack erupted along with a scream.

Everyone turned to see Roger with his arm extended, firearm at the ready. A tiny plume of smoke came out of the tip of the gun. "He's down." He turned around. "Is everyone alright?"

Bernard walked over to the writhing man down on the concrete. He kicked the 9mm out of his reach. "Did you think you were going to grease me? You stupid bastard. You're lucky my boy was the one who shot you. If it was me, your death would've been slow." He patted Roger on the shoulder and looked back. "Take care of this trash, Mr. Edward."

Eddy brushed past Bernard and knelt by the body. He looked down the nearby alley and pointed. "We've got to stash his carcass in that dumpster for now. Help me get him over there, will you? We're just lucky this shithole neighborhood doesn't have cameras. Thank your little tech girl for scouting this place out."

Roger bent down and grabbed the other side. "Ready."

"Go." Eddy strained.

They both lifted the still groaning man. Daniel dashed down the alleyway and opened the dumpster.

Roger grunted. "He didn't look this heavy."

"They never do until after." Eddy looked over his shoulder. "I'm more concerned with that pool of blood back there and the trail we're leaving."

They reached the receptacle. Daniel grabbed a hold and helped them toss him inside. He reached into his back pocket and retrieved his phone. His thumb danced across the screen. "Don't worry. For one thing, the raining should obscure the blood. Two, I'm texting in a cleanup crew as we speak. They'll be here inside of fifteen minutes. We'll be long gone by then." He reached up and slammed the lid down.

Eddy slapped the back of Roger and took off into a jog toward the van. "Let's go, killer."

Roger gave a lingering look at the dumpster. The corners of his mouth fell. A shade of his normal voice came out. "Right behind you." He scampered into the vehicle and shut the door behind him.

Back at Headquarters...

"You should have been there. My boy was the only one who was watching the guy as we were getting ready to leave. Then pow." Eddy raised his thumb and index finger imitating a gun firing. "He saved all our asses." He glanced left. "Hey, there he is. Rog, get over here." He beckoned him over.

Roger approached the small group and sat down at the end of the sofa. "What's up?"

"I was just regaling these slackers here with what you did earlier."

"I'm not exactly proud of that."

The man to his left spoke up immediately. "You should be. I wish it had been me. If only I could prove to the boss how valuable I am." He stared off over Roger's shoulder with a sigh.

"That would require you to actually do something," Eddy laughed. "For real though, good job. I'm proud to know you. That makes twice now you've saved my life. Don't think I'll forget that. Before I forget, I heard Daniel wants to see you."

"You have any idea where he is?" Roger asked.

A wide grin graced Eddy's features as the toothpick danced left and right. He took the toothpick out and used it to point through a door on the far side of the room. "I heard he's with our resident tech division leader. I'd be careful if I were you. Their arguments can sometimes get heated."

"Good to know. Nice to meet you two. I've got to get going. Duty calls and all."

"Good luck. Just remember not to get in between them," Eddy laughed as Roger walked off.

Roger pushed open the door and entered a familiar hallway. He looked out large windows on his left as he passed by. He heard elevated voices as he approached Tanya's workplace. A female voice called out from behind the door.

"Do you even listen when I explain? I swear, you don't even try. You just complain when it doesn't work. Then guess who has to listen to that? Me."

A deeper voice made itself known. "You're the one who

made it. Who the hell else am I going to go ask? The janitor?"

Roger shook his head then knocked on the door.

He heard both voices. "What is it?"

He cracked the door open and peeked inside. Tanya sat on her rolling chair, her cheeks puffed out. Daniel stood a few feet in front of her with his arms crossed in front of his chest. "I was called here, wasn't I? I don't want to interrupt."

"It took you long enough." Daniel turned away from Tanya and made for the door. "I'm done with you if you can't see reason."

"Reason? You want reason? Don't give it to your sister to apply. She breaks everything she touches, just like you. You should have had Rog there handle it. He knows his shit."

Daniel pivoted back to her and held up a lone index finger. He spoke through clenched teeth. "I get it already. Alright?"

Tanya huffed and spun her chair around.

"Be that way, why don't you?" Daniel continued toward the door. He exited and closed it behind him. "Sorry about that. Women, right? How much did you hear?"

"It sounded like the bug didn't quite work as well as we'd hoped."

Daniel strolled down the hallway with Roger at his side. "That's right. Halfway through the meeting it went dead. As you may have heard, our tech genius has her opinions on whose fault it was. Is there any reason you know of that may answer this?"

"It may have gotten wet? Moisture is usually the leading cause for a listening device failing. Of course mechanical failure is also still on the table. I'd have to inspect it to get a better idea, sir."

"I tasked your old mentor to do just that. You may have

heard her bitching. I wanted to talk to you about something far more important." He stopped in the middle of the silent hallway. "I want you front and center next time."

"Sir?"

Daniel clasped his hands behind him and turned to Roger. "You saved my father's life earlier today. You could make the argument that you saved mine, Eddy's, my sister's, and Bruce's as well. Eddy recommended we give you a bigger chance, along with a bigger cut. Interested?"

"Always, sir."

Daniel reached out and gave a playful slap to Roger's shoulder. "That's what I wanted to hear. Show up outside tomorrow ready to go. We go at midnight. Any questions?"

"What should I prepare for exactly?" Roger asked.

"We're going to give Mr. Alexander exactly what he wants. Bring plenty of ammo and get some body armor from downstairs in the armory If the dumbasses try and charge you, tell them I sent you on a job. They'll give it for free then. We're going after the Enforcers. You, me, Eddy, Elizabeth, and Bruce are going. Liz will stay in the car of course. You're with us. Anything else?"

"Have we scouted out the place? I don't relish the idea of going in blind, with all due respect."

"You've got a pair, don't ya? You think I'd just rush us headlong into hopeless situations or something?"

"I didn't say that."

Daniel threw his head back with a boisterous laugh. "I was joking, Rog. I don't mind a little accountability. It keeps us honest, alive, and free. To answer your question, yes, we have scouted it out. That was the other matter I discussed with our blonde firecracker before you showed up. We have the floor plan and surveillance tapes. We'll go over specifics closer to tomorrow night."

"I understand," Roger said. His voice was tired.

"Don't worry so much about it. I'll make sure we all get back in one piece. Take heart. I've never lost a man under my command."

Roger nodded.

"Look, no offense here, Rog, but you need to project an air of confidence. This quiet frowning crap doesn't send the right message. Puff your chest out, wear a shit eating grin, swagger into rooms, and play the part. Keep this on the down low, but I'm just looking out for you. If you want those guys out there to respect you, then act like a top dog, not a lap dog. If you can't do that, then do the 'quiet hard-ass' thing. Just don't keep this pathetic crap up. You reflect on me, and I will not have that."

"I'm just not exactly used to -"

"Then get used to it. I don't care if you never shot a man before. You have now - twice. Adjust and overcome. If you can't do that, you're nothing but a liability. We rely on you to put your big boy pants on in the morning and strap up your proverbial work boots. You understand?"

Roger cleared his throat. "I understand perfectly."

"Good. Now go get ready. I'd recommend practicing at the shooting range outside. Those revolvers aren't the most accurate, are they, grandpa?"

"Hey now."

"Just messing with you. See you soon, brother."

Back home...

Roger sat down on his bed and gave a sidelong glance at the nightstand beside him. He let out a long sigh and opened the drawer. Reaching inside he retrieved a bag of white powder. He placed the bag at his side and reached down under his bed. He grabbed a metal tray that had a straw and razor blade on top of it and placed the tray on his lap. "He wants me to 'deal with it'? Fine. It's not like I deserve better after what I've done."

He opened the baggie and shook out a small pile of powder. He used the razor to chop the powder and pushed it into thin lines. He grabbed the straw and stuck one end up his nostril. Leaning down he placed the straw above the substance and snorted. The powder disappeared.

He coughed and placed it all back into the nightstand before falling back onto his bed. "Mm," he moaned. "A fella could get used to this." His eyes were closed halfway when a knock at his door interrupted him. He closed his eyes. "Yeah?"

His father's voice came through the door. "Son, we need to have a talk."

"Kinda tired right now, Dad."

"I'm coming in."

Roger opened his eyes when he heard creaking. He saw his father enter the room and move to his bed. He stood above him.

"Get up right now."

"I just got back. I'm tired from work."

"I can believe that considering what I saw earlier on television. It's the weirdest thing, Son. You know that loan we owed Mr. Thomas?"

Roger sat up and scooted back against the wall. His head fell back, looking up at his father. "What about it?"

"Someone busted into his joint, stabbed one of his bodyguards, and shot him. Imagine my shock when I realized this happened that one night you came home late. Then we get a call earlier today from the hospital. It was Mr. Thomas telling us that our debt was canceled along with an apology." His voice raised a few octaves. "I'm not stupid, boy! Were you responsible?"

"I didn't do it."

"Did your Morris associates do it on your behalf? That still counts."

Roger turned away from his father. His neck sagged as he did. "I don't know what you're talking about."

"So that's how it is, huh? You just lie right to my face while you're stoned as can be. I'm disappointed in you. Have fun 'nodding off' or whatever you do for fun." He stomped off toward the door and stopped. "This isn't over. If I find out you were involved, you're going to regret it. Know that." He slammed the door shut, leaving the room silent.

A lone tear rolled down Roger's cheek. More fell as he sniffled. "It'll be fine." He laid down and hugged his knees to his chest. "Everything will be okay." He reached down and raised a blanket over his form. "I'm still a good person. Right?"

5

Roger pushed the door open and strode inside with his chin up. A voice to his right stopped him.

"You seem happy today," Bruce said, leaning against the wall. "Something good happen?"

"Not really. I just feel good today." He raised an eyebrow. "Why?"

Bruce chuckled to himself. "You just looked like a different person walking inside. It's not a bad thing. You actually look like a man now, not a scared child."

"You're lucky I'm in a good mood, or I'd take offense at that."

"I'm just busting your chops." He kicked off the wall and came within a few feet. He looked down and flicked Roger's tie. "I see you still don't know how to dress yourself. A red tie? Really?"

"Not everyone can pull off a purple bow tie like you. Some of us actually have style."

"I'm going to choose to ignore that," the corner of Bruce's mouth went up, "for your own sake."

A smoky female voice caused both men to look to their

left. "There you are." Elizabeth sidled down the stairs and stopped beside Bruce. She placed a hand on his shoulder and gripped. "You haven't been avoiding me have you, dear?"

Roger looked toward the rest of the room and saw men giving surreptitious glances and whispering to each other. He looked back to Bruce. "Sorry, Ms. Morris. I was just holding him up with a little talk. My bad."

She sneered and glared at him. "Just butt out already, you annoyance."

"I think she meant -" Bruce started.

"I can talk for myself." She slapped the back of Bruce's head. "Don't speak unless spoken to."

Bruce growled as he rubbed the wound.

A louder series of whispers echoed across the room.

"You didn't like that?" she asked. "Too bad." She turned to the audience. "Mind your own business, or else."

"We're over. You do remember that conversation, right? What? You can't get that through your thick skull?"

"Oh boy," Roger whispered under his breath.

Elizabeth's normally pale face began reddening. "You have the gall to speak to me like that?"

"You're crazy. Everyone here knows it."

"Hold on now," Roger said. "This doesn't have to -"

"Crazy? You know what?" Elizabeth asked. "I'm through. I don't have to take that from someone like you." She stomped up the stairs. The sound of a door slamming caused the chattering to resume across the lobby.

Roger looked at Bruce. "That could have gone better."

"Are you nuts? I'm free, brother." Bruce pumped his fist. "Come on. Let's go teach you a thing or two before tonight about aiming. The range is just out the back door and then a short hike. You're going to love it. There's no one around for miles. Let's go."

That Night...

Roger reached into his coat pocket and removed a small already half burned paper cylinder and a lighter. He put it between his lips. He placed his hand in front of his face and flicked the lighter. A flame jumped out and engulfed the makeshift joint. A puff of smoke billowed out of the corner of his mouth. "That's the stuff." He brought his left wrist up to eye level. "They'll be ready soon. I should probably hurry this up." The end of the stick glowed a bright orange. He inhaled deeply and coughed out a huge cloud of smoke. The end burned down with every inhale along with more rolling smoke. Once it had reached his fingertips, he dropped it on the pavement and snuffed it out with his heel. He kicked it behind him into the grass.

The front door opened and the small group exited, led by Daniel. He swaggered over until his nose crinkled up. He waved his hand back and forth in front of his face. "What is that?"

"Smells like someone is having a party," Bruce said from the back of the group. He continued sniffing the air. "A really nice party from the smell of it. I'm a little jealous."

"Right," Daniel said in a deadpan tone. He gave a pointed, momentary glare at Roger before brushing past him. "I'm driving." He sat down in the driver's seat and closed the door.

"Oh shit," Bruce said. His hand fell to his stomach. "Does anyone have any motion sickness pills?"

Daniel poked his head out of the open window and looked back. "No. Sack up."

Elizabeth pushed Bruce out of the way and moved toward the backseat. On her way she glanced at Roger out of the corner of her eye. She turned her nose up with a huff. "Hurry up already. We don't have all day."

"Yes, Ma'am," Roger, Bruce, and Eddy said in unison.

Eddy circled around to the passenger side and got into the front seat. Roger followed behind but sat in the backseat.

"Move over." Roger looked to his right and saw Bruce standing.

Roger scooted to his left.

"Be careful. I don't want to touch you," Elizabeth said from his left.

"Aww," Eddy said. "I think she likes the new guy."

A growl escaped Elizabeth's throat. "I've no clue where you got that from."

"Simple," Eddy said. "You acted the same way when you and Bruce got together. You don't remember that?"

Bruce pulled the seat belt across his body. "Yeah, dude. I'd be careful."

"I don't think that -" Roger said before he was interrupted by Daniel.

"We need to focus on the job, not whatever this is." He twisted the key. "He's right though, by the way. You did give him nothing but shit when he was new." He dropped his foot onto the gas pedal and the car lurched forward.

"Because that's what's important right now," Elizabeth said. She looked out the window beside her.

The long silence that followed was interrupted by Daniel flicking the turn signal and rotating the wheel. "Getting serious, everyone did come packing, right? I hope so because tonight is going to be wild."

"What's the plan?" Roger asked.

"Don't you remember? Alexander gave us our MO on a silver platter," Elizabeth sneered.

Bruce leaned forward and looked across Roger's chest. "We weren't inside the building. Don't you remember? How could either of us know what was said in there?"

"We're going to deliver some good old-fashioned gang-land violence," Daniel said. "We're headed to a well-known Enforcer hang out. We take a few out and leave. Simple."

"Drive by?" Eddy asked.

"We'll have to see when we get there, but I doubt it. Unless they're just sitting outside, it's not really reliable." He looked up into the rear-view mirror. "Liz will be watching the car. Rog, you're going with Eddy this time." His eyes darted to his right before returning to the road. "That alright with you?"

"Of course," Eddy said. "We'll deal with them. Just you watch."

"Of that I have no doubt," Daniel said.

"In fact," Eddy said, "I'll bet you a grand we'll bag more than you and Bruce."

Bruce kicked the seat in front of him. "Bull. There's no way you and Mister Six Shooter here can compare to the semi-automatics we're packing. Logistics, and logic for that matter, will see to that."

Elizabeth rolled her eyes and exhaled. "Boys and their egos." She stole a peek at Roger beside her. "I at least thought you'd be better than them."

"Did you hear that? She believed in the new guy? I told ya she was interested in him," Eddy cackled.

"It's time to get serious, boys." Daniel's foot pushed the brakes. "We're here. I don't see anyone outside."

"What a mess of a bar," Elizabeth said. "That tacky neon sign in the window sure isn't doing them any favors. I'm pretty sure I can see a crack in the glass too. Do these people not even try?"

"I doubt they're designers, Sis," Daniel said. He reached down into his belt line and removed his pistol. "Bruce and I will take the front. You and Eddy circle around and head in the back."

"We're sure it has a back door?" Roger asked. "The last thing we want is for you two to be left hanging in there. What am I saying? Of course you know. You do have the floor plans don't you?"

"He's got a point, buddy. Just because the plans say they have a backdoor doesn't mean they have one," Eddy said.

"Fire regulations dictate they need an alternate exit, doesn't it? If they didn't, they'd have been shut down. Also, yes, I'm sure jackass."

"Not to be a wet blanket here," Roger said, "but they could have bribed past that inconvenience, couldn't they? I doubt it undergoes yearly inspections."

Bruce grunted beside him. "He's got a point."

"I don't give a shit if they bribed someone. They have a back door - period. You two go first if you're so worried. Just give us a signal when you're ready."

"Nice going, you dolt," Elizabeth giggled. "Try not to die."

"Aww," Eddy cooed. "She's wishing him good luck now."

"God dammit, just get out of here already," Elizabeth spat.

Out back of the bar...

"At least we're not going in the front," Roger said. "That's something at least."

"Yeah," Eddy smirked. "We'll get loads of action back here, if I'm right." He pointed ahead of the pair toward a graffiti marked back door. "There's our ticket. Now go and let them know we're ready."

"Got it." Roger turned around and dashed off. He stayed near the side of the building and peeked around the brick corner. He saw the van parked across the street. He raised a lone thumb up.

He heard two doors slam and dashed back to Eddy. "They're on their way." He reached into his jacket and pulled out the two revolvers. "When do we go anyway?"

"Trust me. We'll know."

A piercing crack, along with a symphony of screams, interrupted their discussion.

"We go now," Eddy said. He opened the door and ducked inside.

Roger followed behind. He saw Eddy in front of him with his back to a dingy graffiti stained wall, facing him. A small path to the right led out into the main room.

"Keep your head down. When they reload, we catch them in the back. Simple enough. Right? Just remember to aim low."

"You don't have to tell me twice." Roger hurled himself across the opening. He angled his head down and landed on his shoulders. He rolled forward, stopped, and placed his back on the other side of the funnel.

"Did the rolling help?" Eddy asked over the cacophony.

Roger patted himself down. "No extra holes, so I think so."

The building went quiet, aside from faint sniveling and crying, until a loud voice cried out. "They're out."

Eddy cocked his pistol. "Time to go to work." He swiveled around the corner and unloaded.

Roger peeked around and saw overturned tables, people lying on the ground clutching their various wounds, and three armed men wearing yellow bandanas facing the front. They periodically peeked over their makeshift cover of tables and squeezed off a few rounds. He could see the end of a shotgun pointing at the front above the bar on their left. He pivoted around the corner and took aim at the ones he flanked and squeezed both triggers. His arms bucked back.

The closest fell forward onto the table with an audible squelch as liquid crimson pooled beneath him. The same voice as before called out. "Shit, they're flanking us. They're in the back."

Eddy returned behind cover. He ejected the magazine and slid another in. He looked over. "I was the one who got him."

Roger ducked behind the wall. The wall in front of them was now beginning to have holes appear in it. He flicked the cylinder open and emptied the spent cartridges onto the floor. He refilled them one at a time. "I challenge that ruling."

Eddy angled his arm around the corner and squeezed off a few rounds in a blind fire. "I sure hope we get relieved soon. It is starting to get a little dicey back here in the broom closet. I think we've almost got them all though."

The building fell dead silent. No gunfire, no groaning, no sound came. Eddy peeked around the corner. "Cover me. I'm finishing this." He hunched over and turned the corner. He stayed low, keeping the bar on his left. "Get the car ready," he shouted toward the front.

"Shit," Roger muttered under his breath. "Why me?" he asked. He sneaked forward and caught up. He poked Eddy's shoulder and whispered. "There's a shotgun just to our left behind the bar. Careful now."

"I've got it. Watch and learn." Eddy flicked the hand from his shoulder and crept ahead. He readied his weapon and faced the surface to his left. He stood and squeezed the trigger. A mist of blood and a gurgling howl filled the air. He peered over the bar, turned around, and cupped a hand to his mouth. "Coast is clear, gentlemen. Come on inside."

Daniel's head peaked out from the front door frame. "I'm not so sure about that. I think there was one more."

Eddy surveyed the room and shrugged. He waved him in. "There's no one else here, boss."

A door slammed open, and a gunshot sounded. A splatter of blood later, Eddy was backing away. He stumbled into the middle of the room, his right hand clutching his abdomen. He crumpled to the floor and writhed around on the already stained hardwood.

Roger crept forward until he was stopped by Daniel's booming voice. "Hold your fucking position in there!"

Roger watched Eddy roll over and face him. He shook his head left and right. He glanced up at Daniel's position. "Screw it," he whispered to himself. He raised his voice. "Cover me."

"What?" Daniel asked. "I said hold."

"Court martial me later why don't you? I'm not leaving him out there." Roger holstered the revolver in his left hand.

"Fine, hero. The shooter is to your left, behind the pinball machine. I've got him pinned down. Go."

Roger dashed forward. He reached and grasped Eddy's hand in his left. "Hold on, buddy. I've got you." He glanced to his left and fired a shot across his body. He pulled Eddy, a trail of red following them, until they reached the cover of the bar. He propped Eddy's back against it and leaned forward to inspect him. "Oh no."

"How bad is it?" Eddy's voice was raspy.

Roger's eyes lingered on the wound and danced up to Eddy's eyes. "You'll be fine. Just keep pressure on it. We'll get you out of here." He took his suit jacket off and shoved it into Eddy's hands. "Use this."

"What are you waiting on? Get out of there." Daniel angled around the door frame and fired off another slug. He cocked the shotgun and fired off another round. "Hurry up. We're leaving."

"That's damned right you are," an unfamiliar voice said. "You Morris boys think this is over? This is war."

Roger reached down and looped Eddy's left arm over his neck. "You heard the boss." He strained as they stood up. His right arm held the formal attire against his newly received wound as tightly as he could manage. "We've worn out our welcome." He took an unsteady step back where they'd come from. "You're heavy. Anyone ever told you that?"

"Bite me."

The pair hobbled out of the back door and circled around the building. They came to the front. "On your left," Roger said.

Daniel fired another shell inside. He pumped the shotgun and brought it up to his shoulder. "Get him in the van. I'll cover us." The rifle kicked with another squeeze of the trigger.

Roger hauled Eddy across the street. "Where the hell's Bruce?"

"Who knows?" Eddy said at his side.

They reached the van. Roger slid the back door open. "Get in the back. I need this seat."

"Who do you think -" She stopped when she saw Eddy's head hanging at his side. She raised a hand to her mouth and gasped. "Oh my God."

"Help me get him in there and then get in the back," Roger said, louder this time. He shoved Eddy onto the seat.

Elizabeth got out the other side and circled around the car. She threw open the doors and climbed in the back. She crawled over to the seat and got on her knees. "What happened?" Her eyes fell. "Where's your jacket? For that matter, why is the building on fire now?"

"Right here, doll face," Eddy coughed. He rolled onto his back. Blood dribbled down his chin. "I think he got me in the stomach, judging from the blood."

"They're burning the building down and evacuating." Daniel hopped into the driver's seat. "It works for us. Your DNA will be burned away, buddy."

Roger placed his weight on the field dressing. "I think that was the other guy's blood. You remember? The guy with the shotgun. You were like five feet away. This doesn't look too bad."

"Are you nuts?" Elizabeth asked.

"You're not a very good liar, Rog." Eddy reached out and seized Roger's forearm. "I like that about you."

Roger pushed down on his chest. "Take it easy. You'll get out of this alive. Trust me."

Daniel looked back. "Where's Bruce? I lost him after it started."

"Don't ask me. I've no idea," Roger said, still applying pressure. "He was gone when we got here. You may want to ask your sister."

More footsteps clattered on the asphalt outside. Daniel reached down his pants, pulled out his 9mm, and leveled it at the passenger's side door.

The door sprung open. Bruce hopped in and slammed the door behind him. He panted, sweat rolling down his brows. "Let's go."

"No arguments here," Daniel said with a twist of the key. He stepped on the gas. "Where were you?"

"I went around the side and got some shots off through a window. Why?"

"Look behind you," Daniel said with a growl.

Bruce turned around in his seat. His eyes went wide. His voice shook. "Eddy?"

Daniel's voice became louder. "He's shot in the gut it looks like. Call the doc and tell him to meet us back at the house." He looked over. "Now, jackass."

Bruce was shaken from his stunned silence. "Right. Got it." He dug his hands into his pockets and fished out his phone. He dialed a number and raised it to his ear. "Get over to the house. Now! We've had an injury that requires your services." He paused. "That's probably safe to assume. It's a stomach wound. Hurry up."

"Where were you, really?" Daniel asked.

"What?" Bruce asked.

Daniel looked up into the rear-view mirror. "Maybe I should just ask you, Sis. Where was he? You had a clear view, didn't you?"

Elizabeth bit her lip and looked down at Eddy's writhing form.

"Don't want to answer, huh? I can make a pretty good guess. You brought him back here, and you two tried to make up while we were fighting for our lives. Am I right? At least have the balls to admit it."

"Leave it be, Danny." Eddy gurgled and coughed. He leaned his head over the side of the seat and looked to the front. "This isn't helping. Do it later. Keep your cool. You're the leader right now. Remember that."

Daniel took a deep breath and cast a glance over to Bruce. "I'll deal with you later."

"Tough luck for Brucie," Eddy moaned. "The princess here has the hots for my nurse. He's missed that boat." He craned his neck and looked up at Elizabeth. "Ain't that right, sweetie?"

Elizabeth brought a hand up and scratched her nose. She looked down at the back of Roger's head. "He's delirious. We need to hurry. Just be careful not to speed too much, Bro. Besides," she smirked, "if he's still got the energy to joke around, he's fine for a while yet." She reached down and flicked the back of Roger's neck. "Be careful down there. Don't let him move too much. Don't you know anything about treating people?"

"Because you're the queen of sensitivity, right?" Roger asked.

"He finally fights back," Daniel chuckled. "Better late than never."

6

Roger sat down on the side of his sister's bed. He looked down and saw her looking up at him, holding her favorite teddy bear.

She removed a hand from the polyester animal and pinched her nose. "You smell weird again. Did you do that stuff that Dad told you not to again or something?"

"Sorry about that. Work was hard today. I haven't had a chance to take a shower yet, munchkin." He rubbed her head, messing up her flowing auburn hair.

"Work was hard?" Her voice fell to a ghost of its former self. "Is that why Daddy still hasn't got a job yet?"

"Shh." Roger placed a hand over his sister's mouth. "Quiet about that. He's doing his best."

Her eyes widened and she clamped a tiny hand over her mouth after Roger removed his. She nodded her head and removed her hand. "Okay."

"After the last incident he had at the welding place, it's hard for him to find work. But I know he will. He never gives up. It's what you have to do in life."

She reached down and pulled the covers up over her legs. "That doesn't sound like very much fun."

"It's not," he said, "but it's what everyone has to do. If we didn't, we'd all lose our houses and go hungry. It's the way of the world."

She brought a hand to her mouth and coughed into it. "The world sounds hard," she said. "Why can't it be fun?"

"Sometimes it is," Roger said. "That's one thing I hope you learn from me. Don't be like me and go only for money. When you grow up, I want you to follow your interests. Find a job you love and enjoy doing. It's not work then."

"I heard Dad tell Mom I might not." She leaned into his side.

"Might not?" Roger asked. His eyes widened. His arm fell and enveloped her in a hug. "Don't listen to him. He's not a doctor. In fact, I'm working on getting you a new medicine as we speak. Your brother won't let anything happen to you. You know that."

She looked up at him with puppy dog eyes. "What does it do?"

"It's supposed to improve your lung function. It means it'd be easier to breathe, and you wouldn't be coughing as much. Does that sound like something you'd be interested in? I'm planning on getting the money so we can ask your doctor about it later. Sound good?"

She leaned away from him and bounced on the springy bed. "It sure does," she said with a beaming smile. She reached over and wrapped her arms around him. "I love you, Bub."

He returned the gesture and placed a hand on the back of her head. "Love you too." He pushed her away with ease. "The first step to getting better is going to bed halfway early.

You do your part, and I'll do mine." He extended a palm toward her. "Deal?"

She clasped his hand and squeezed. "Yep."

"Good." He reached over to the nightstand and grabbed the mask and vibration coat. He handed them over to his sister. "You know the drill."

"I hate these things," she said with a pout. She reached up and adjusted the mask over her nose. "They always get in the way while I'm asleep."

A sharp knock at the door caused them both to look over. Their father's voice could be heard. "Time for bed, Michelle. You know the rules." The door squeaked open. He entered the room and stopped. "I didn't know your brother was in here. We were looking for him." He shook his head. "You used the ladder into your room again, didn't you? How many times do we have to tell you that's not safe, Son?"

Roger's gaze never moved from his sister. "I didn't want to risk waking everyone up is all."

"Uh huh." Keith narrowed his eyes, sighed, and looked over to Michelle. "I see you're done in here, so come downstairs before bed." He moved out of the room and poked his head back in. "That's not a question by the way."

"I got it," Roger said.

Keith closed the door behind him, leaving the two alone.

"Bub," Michelle said, "is everything okay? Are you in trouble? I'll help."

"It's nothing that I didn't bring on myself. Don't you worry about it. I'll take care of it. They probably just want to ask me a few questions about my work."

Michelle released a hacking wheeze, causing the mask to fog up. "What do you do for work anyway? You've never told me."

Roger scratched his nose and looked out the window

across the room. "I'm in..." he paused, "acquisitions. Basically, the boss tells me to go get something, and I do. Simple enough. Right?"

"You're lying, aren't you? I can tell. Is that why they're mad? Are you lying to them too? You always told me to tell the truth to Mom and Dad."

Roger looked down into his sister's eyes and gave a wide smile. "Maybe I am. You won't know until you're older." He stood up from the bed and pulled the covers up over her shoulders. "Besides, there's always an exception to every rule. They're just rare." He moved to the door and opened it. "Get some sleep, Sis. Let your brother take care of everything. You just rest."

"Okay." She hugged her favorite polyester bear to her chest and closed her eyes.

Downstairs...

"It took you long enough," Keith said.

Roger trudged down the stairs. "Yeah?" He reached the bottom of the stairs and turned the corner, only to find his mother standing there with her arms crossed. "Let me guess."

"You don't have to," Beatrice said. "Your father told me everything that's happened the past few days." She stepped forward and grabbed Roger's ear, causing him to bend over. Her voice escalated as she spoke into his ear. "Did you think we wouldn't find out? A man is in the hospital now, and you're involved. Why? For simple money? Is that all? For God's sake, you could be put in prison for this? Have you even thought of that?"

"He never listens, Bea." Keith placed a hand on Beatrice's hand and removed it from Roger's ear. "He just loves hanging out with them Morris boys for a little scratch."

"That's rich coming from you," Roger said, "lest we forget the last time and the dozens before. You want to air dirty laundry? I've got more than enough on you, old man."

Beatrice backed out of Keith's embrace. "What does he mean?"

"You don't know?" Roger asked with a grin. "Shall we go on, Father?"

"Be quiet, boy. I wouldn't have imagined you'd go from assault to blackmail in so short a time. What's happened to you?"

"Oh no, no, no. If we're going to be truthful, let's get it all out in the open, Dad. You want my whole paycheck to avoid telling Ma?" He reached into his back pants pocket and pulled out his wallet. He opened it and thumbed through the bills. "You drained me the last time. I mean, obviously you didn't hold up your end of the bargain, but is all of my money still the deal?"

Beatrice shoved Keith back and backed away. "You hid this from me? You knew what he was doing? How could you lie to me like that? What happened to always telling each other the truth?"

"That's not what's important right now, honey." Keith stomped his foot and pointed at Roger. "He's the one hurting people here."

"He's not the only one," Beatrice said. She glanced back at Roger. "As for you, you're not denying it?"

"I'm doing what I have to for this family. Someone has to pay for Michelle's medicine, don't they?" He glared at his father.

"That doesn't justify this." Beatrice shook her head. "Just

tell them you quit and come back home. It's not too late, Son." She took a step forward and pulled his head into her shoulder. "You're still my boy, and I love you. I'll always love you. Come back home and get a real job."

Roger stood with his hands at his side. He spoke, muffled into his mother's shoulder. "I can't. It's not possible."

Beatrice released him and placed her palms on her hips. Her head tilted as she spoke. "What do you mean, 'I can't'?"

"The only way out for me is..." he paused and looked away. "I just can't. I don't expect you to understand. Just know it's not possible for me."

Beatrice brought a hand up to her mouth. Tears started glistening in her eyes, threatening to fall. "What have you done for them? You didn't...?" She gasped. Salty drops trailed down her cheeks.

Roger stared at his shoes. "Whatever you're thinking, the answer is probably yes. Now you see why they won't let me leave." His voice cracked. "I'm in too deep. I'm sorry. Your son's a failure."

"No, I won't believe it," Beatrice gasped. "Not my boy. We raised you to be a good Christian. How could you?" She backed up until her back hit the stairwell. She covered her face with her hands as she moaned.

"How deep are we talking here, Son?" Keith asked. "You don't mean like erasing a guy?"

Beatrice latched onto Keith. "There's no way our son would take another man's life. He knows the commandments."

"Son? Are you going to answer me? Or do I have to go and take it up with your superiors? You know I will."

"I wouldn't recommend it," Roger said.

"Then tell us what you've done."

"I can't."

Keith removed Beatrice's arms from around his waist and went toe to toe with his son. He placed both hands on Roger's shoulders. "Tell me. I'm not the best dad I admit, but I will do anything to get you out of this." He squeezed his hands, causing Roger to flinch. "It's that, or I go ask them directly? Is that what you'd rather I do?"

Beatrice's shaky breath interrupted her husband. "He's basically admitted to it already, honey. He never denied killing a man. Didn't you notice? He just refused to answer."

Keith returned his glance to Roger's downcast face. "Is that true?" He shook him. "Is it true? Did you?" He backed away, shaking his head. "It is true. You're a murderer, aren't you?"

Roger turned his back to them. "I've done what I've had to for this family."

"Get out," Keith's quiet voice said.

Beatrice pawed at Keith's chest. "Keith, no. He's still our little boy no matter what happens."

"You heard him, dear. He doesn't deny it. You know what will happen if we let him stay here? I'll tell you. He'll bring more and more of that stuff around here. Eventually it'll affect us. Maybe Michelle up there might get mixed in with him. I'm not willing to take that chance. He's lying in bed with the devil, and I don't want him infecting the rest of us with his lifestyle choices. What if another gang retaliates against him with a drive-by? You or Michelle might be killed. I cannot allow that. He has to go."

Roger lifted a foot and climbed the stairs. "At least let me go talk to Michelle before I leave. I need to pack."

"Hurry up, Mr. Gangster. I want you out of here within the hour."

"I got it," Roger said as he climbed the stairs. His voice fell to a whisper. "Jackass." He reached the top of the stairs, looked left through the wooden guard rails, and saw Michelle standing there with her bear hanging at her side. His eyes softened. "How much did you hear?"

"You're leaving?" She snorted and wiped her eyes clear of tears. "Why? Why is Dad doing this?"

Roger turned the corner and knelt in front of his sister. "He's doing what he thinks is best for you. Honestly, he might be right."

"No." She shook her head. "I don't want you to leave."

He pulled her head onto his shoulder and whispered into her ear. "I don't want to leave you either." He pulled back and looked her in the eyes. "Promise me you'll put the equipment on every night, especially when dad forgets. Promise?"

She snorted and brought a small hand up to wipe her nose. "That's your job, Bub."

"Not anymore. It's yours now. Just remember what I'd make you do, and do it. No cheating. Otherwise you'll make me worry. You don't want that, do you?"

"No," her timid voice said. She looked up at him. "Will you call or email me?"

"Every night I can. I promise." Roger stood up and nodded toward his door. "Come on. Want to help your big bro pack?"

"Not really," she said with a wipe of her eyes, "but I will."

Roger placed a hand on her shoulder. "That's my girl." He guided them into his room...

Out in front of the house...

"Who's in that car?" Keith asked from inside the open doorway.

"My ride," Roger said. He shrugged under the strap of the backpack over his shoulder. "I guess you could say he's my boss. I assumed you weren't going to let me take the car. Was I right?"

"Obviously," Keith said. "So that's where you're going to shack up? With them?"

"What other choice do I have exactly?" Roger asked.

The car across the street honked its horn. "If you'll excuse me, I think he's getting impatient." He turned away from them. "Take care of Michelle." He walked down the steps onto the grass.

A splitting voice caused him to pause. A torrent of footsteps accompanied the voice. "Hold on a minute." Michelle bounded down the stairs barefoot and pushed past her parents.

Roger dropped his handheld bag to the ground, opened his arms and caught her in an embrace.

"You forgot something. Here." She slipped the paper in her hand into one of his jacket pockets. "Be careful," she said.

"What was that?" Roger asked, pulling away from the embrace and picking up the bag.

"My online information. You always forget." She backed up until Keith pulled her back behind him.

He planted a hand on her shoulder as he spoke. "Get back inside. It's too cold out here for you, honey."

"I just wanted to say bye to Bub," she said. She peeked around her father and waved.

Beatrice grabbed her hand, pulled her up the steps, and back inside the house. "Obey your father, and get back in bed. You have school tomorrow," she glanced back at Roger, "unlike some people."

A thundering clack drew everyone's attention to the car waiting. A familiar figure approached the house.

Daniel strode forward and came to a stop halfway to the house. "Yo, you ready? I haven't got all night. It's already nine." He turned to the house. "Is that your family?"

"Yeah. My bad." Roger turned away from the house. "I was just saying goodbye. I'm through."

Daniel raised a hand in the direction of the house. "Good. Let's get out of here. Wait a minute. Did you see that? I think your father just flipped me off. He's got some sack, doesn't he?"

Roger looked over and confirmed his father was indeed giving the one finger salute in their direction. "Ignore his dumb ass. He's the one who got me kicked out."

"Because of us, huh? Well, he gets a pass since he's your dad. If anyone else had, you know what I'd have done?"

"Broken his fingers?" Roger asked.

"Close." He placed a hand on Roger's shoulder, turned him away from the house, and walked back to the car. "Why take out a lone finger when you can just break their wrist? It hurts much worse, don't you know?

"I don't think that's common knowledge, sir."

"That's how you get respect in this world, Rog - by showing you're not a limp wristed noodle boy that others can push around. You stick with me and I'll teach you all kinds of things. Just chuck those bags in the back and we'll go."

Roger circled around the car, opened the passenger door, and climbed inside. He tossed the bag into the back seat, extricated himself from the backpack and tossed it beside it.

Daniel got into the driver's seat, slammed the door shut, and twisted the key in the ignition. "Here's the first lesson. Don't let anyone screw with you. Establish dominance, and then you're the one in control. Make sense?" He leaned back and gestured toward the house. "I'm suspecting you've already taken my advice with this issue."

"With all due respect, sir, it cost me my family."

"That's where you're partly wrong. You've also gained one. Always remember that." He stepped on the gas and continued talking. "There's a couple of things I've been wanting to talk to you about."

Roger rubbed his eyes with a yawn. "Yes?"

"First," Daniel started, "Eddy will be fine, in no small part thanks to you. I respect and even admire what you did in there. There's just one small problem."

"I imagine I can guess what it is."

"You disobeyed a direct order." Daniel glanced over at his passenger and back to the road. "Ordinarily that'd be a major fubar, but considering what you did for Eddy..." he trailed off and cleared his throat. "I'll let it pass this time." His voice hardened. "Just don't make a habit of it again. Are we clear?"

"Crystal. I just couldn't leave him out there to die, sir."

"I know, kid." Daniel said. "I understand perfectly. He's one of my best friends. Know that I appreciate it almost as much as he does. Just don't think that gives you a blank check."

"Understood."

"There's one more thing." Daniel leaned over and sniffed. "Yep. I knew it. That smell before we left was you, wasn't it? What is it? Weed? Cigarettes?"

Roger rubbed his wrists and looked at his lap. "I, well..."

"It was herb, wasn't it? Look, I don't care for the stuff. So long as you can shoot straight and keep a clear head, it's fine with me. The moment it becomes a problem, then you're done. No more, period. I can't argue with the bravery you showed. Whether that was due to inebriation or genuine heroism doesn't matter a bit to me. Results are all that matters in this line of work. Just remember if anyone asks, you're clean. Got it?"

"I'll keep that in mind."

His fingertips tapped the top of the steering wheel. "Which reminds me, I need a volunteer now that Eddy is out of commission for a while. You up for it?"

"I'm always up for a payday, sir," Roger said with a grin.

"That's what I like to hear. Get out of that hoodie and into your suit when we get back to your new home. Oh, and call me Daniel."

7

"I'm going to go get Bruce. You go get my sister and rendezvous with us in the meeting room. I'll explain everything there. She should be in her room. Do you know where that is?"

"It's where I first ran into her. I think I can manage."

"Good. I'll meet you in fifteen minutes then." Daniel walked ahead and exited through a nearby door on the first floor.

Roger looked left at the men sitting on the nearby sofa watching the widescreen television. He shook his head and sighed as they cheered along with the sports announcer's yelling. "I wish I still had time for stuff like that." He climbed the familiar staircase and entered the double doors. He saw a man standing at the door at the far end of the hallway. He walked halfway down the corridor and stopped in front of the door where he'd seen Bruce exit before. He raised an arm and knocked on the cherry oak.

Elizabeth's voice could be heard. "Just a minute."

He heard shuffling inside until the door opened.

Elizabeth eyed him up and down. "Yeah? What do you

want? If this is about Bruce, just save it. I'm through with that jackass."

Roger raised an eyebrow. "No. Your brother asked me to get you and for us to report for a meeting."

She placed a palm on the door frame and leaned against it. "What for? I haven't heard of anything going down."

"You've got me. I just heard about it myself."

"I heard a funny story." The corner of Elizabeth's mouth curved upward. "The rumor going around is that you got kicked out of your parents' tonight. I didn't take you for a mama's boy."

"With all due respect, Ms. Morris, you have no idea what happened."

"Enlighten me then."

"Maybe later if you're still interested. For now we have somewhere we need to be, or your brother will have my head."

Elizabeth's lips contorted into a pout. "Aw, you're no fun." She pushed off the door frame. "Fine. Just answer me one thing before we head off."

Roger took a step back, allowing Elizabeth to step into the hallway. "What's that?"

"Why did it happen?"

Roger reached up and massaged his temples. "They learned what I've done."

"Ooh, how cryptic," Elizabeth said with a gesture of her hands. "Am I going to get any more than that?"

"Let's just say that they didn't approve of my methods of providing for my sister."

"I didn't know you had a sister." She closed the door and leaned back against it. "Doesn't your mom or dad have a job?"

"I appreciate the interest, but we're going to be late at

this rate, Ms. Morris. No offense, but I don't want to piss your brother off."

She giggled. "He always has been one of those sticklers for punctuality. Fine. I'm not done with you yet though, Mr. Johnson. Remember that for next time."

He extended an arm toward the door leading to the lobby. "After you."

"At least someone here has manners. You've no clue how rare that is." Her high heels clacked on the hardwood floor as she sashayed her way in front of him. She turned around with a sharp tone in her voice. "Where were you looking?"

His eyes raised and locked with hers. "I don't think there's a right answer here."

She brought a hand up to her mouth and stifled a laugh. "Correct."

Ten minutes later...

Roger sat in the front row of the fold-up chairs, all the way at the end. Elizabeth flanked him, with Bruce on her other side.

Roger gave a sideways glance at the former pair. Bruce kept stealing looks in her direction. Every time Elizabeth caught his gaze, she sneered and leaned away from him.

Elizabeth's shoulder touched Roger's. She paused, making sure Bruce caught a good look. "Stop looking over here already."

Bruce shrugged. "You don't have to tell me twice. I just feel sorry for Rog over there. It looks like he's lost his personal space is all."

"Is that right? I didn't know you had such a bleeding

heart. Besides, he doesn't mind it. A real gentleman accommodates - something you never grasped."

Bruce looked away at the door on the opposite side. "I'm just looking out for the new guy is all. Someone has to."

The door opened, slamming into the wall with a thunderous boom. Daniel sauntered inside and closed it behind him. He moved behind the podium in the middle of the room and looked down at the clipboard in his hands. "Quiet down, girls." He looked up and craned his neck to the right. "Why are you all over there? Never mind." He flipped the clipboard so they could all see the paper. "Our last operation was a resounding success, aside from Eddy getting clipped."

The page showed a picture of Ronald Alexander in front of a collection of microphones with the headlines "Alexander to crack down on firearm violence if elected."

Daniel tapped the paper. "Our benefactor is getting all kinds of support for his reform. Let's keep the momentum going. After all, the election's in just a few days."

Elizabeth yawned. "What's the plan already, Brother? You're boring us to death here."

"For those with an attention span of a goldfish, the plan is simple. We're going to go raise some more hell. This time we're going to a more affluent community." He smiled. "There's no leader of civic reform like a bunch of pissed off rich people."

"They're the ones that cry to the politicians to pass laws. Right?" Bruce asked. He rubbed his mustache. "It seems like a great idea. Who are we going after?"

"We're knocking off Thurgooden's."

Elizabeth leaned forward. "Ooh, I've always wanted a few of their dresses. They charge an arm and a leg."

Roger raised his hand. "I assume this will be after hours?"

"Ordinarily, yes. We'd just take out the alarms and go in quietly. This time, no. The whole point of this is to cause mass panic to the public. We must go in just before closing. Late enough so that there's not a ton of people, but early enough to really get the rumor mill going."

"Won't they have silent alarms?" Roger asked. "We'll need to get in and out in a hurry."

Daniel snapped his fingers and pointed at Roger. "Exactly. We'll put on our masks, gloves, and all that. Then we'll go in, point some guns at their faces, and get out. No one has to die, which is better for staying under the radar anyway. We'll get away with a wad of money, help Mr. Alexander, and be away before anyone even realizes it."

"If one of their security resists our withdrawal?" Bruce asked with a thumb on his chin.

"If any rent-a-cops interfere, we put them down. That'll reinforce the whole 'guns are a public threat' narrative. The most they should have is a taser anyway. The place restricts guns on the premises. You know what that means."

"We're the only ones armed in there," Roger said. "Why not just put up a sign asking to be robbed?"

"I believe they did," Elizabeth said.

Daniel placed the clipboard down and clutched the sides of the podium. "And we won't neglect their plea. Everyone arm up, and we'll be off. They close in a couple of hours, so don't delay too long."

Outside Thurgooden's...

Daniel pulled on a black ski mask. He looked to his left at Bruce's dark blue mask. "Alright, everyone cool?" He investigated the back seat and saw Roger's red mask, along with Elizabeth's gray, staring back at him. "Close enough. Everyone ready?"

"I don't think we have much choice, sir." Roger looked down at his phone. "We have around ten minutes left before they close."

Bruce pointed out the front window. "Boss? Look over there. That limousine looks mighty familiar."

Roger placed his hands on the headrests and leaned forward. "Holy crap, that's Ronald Alexander's car. Is he in there at this time of night?"

Daniel pulled out his pistol and cocked it before shoving it down the front of his pants. "That's all the better. The future mayor is about to get a lot of good publicity. He'll be victimized the same as his voter base. They'll eat that up I bet. Just remember, he's off limits. At most, give him a black eye. You know, for credibility's sake."

"Reporters would love to hear the story of an up-and-coming mayor fighting off the evil criminals," Roger said.

"We're going to give it to them. Bruce, you go make sure that dipshit bodyguard doesn't get brave while we do our thing." Daniel reached over and opened the door beside him. "Let's go already. Stay off the main street. We'll meet inside. After that, Bruce, you stay in the car. You can manage that can't you? Or are you going to wander off in the middle of a goddamned operation again?"

Elizabeth reached forward and slapped her brother's shoulder. "I am not staying behind with him. Not again."

"Again?" Roger asked, looking at her beside him.

Daniel's eyes jumped from his sister and landed on Bruce. "I guess we finally have confirmation where you were." He looked back at his sister. "You're with us. Just don't shoot anybody. Follow my lead."

"I can handle myself," Elizabeth growled. "You just focus on the rest."

"I'm serious, Liz," Daniel said, his voice stern. "Stay behind Rog. Shit is going to get real in there."

Elizabeth gave a toothy smile toward Roger. "I guess you're my bodyguard now."

Bruce blinked, staring into the rear-view mirror. "I never thought I'd see the day you'd graciously accept protection."

"Well, why not? He's already saved my life once. What did you ever do except bitch anyway?"

"Excuse me," Roger said, interrupting them. "I think it's time to go."

"Exactly," Daniel barked. "Lock and load." He pushed the door further open and stepped out, slamming it behind him. He circled around the car, opening the trunk, and extricating his signature shotgun. He took off into a jog toward the store and ducked into a nearby alley.

"I guess we're following him then," Roger said with a reach toward the door handle. He looked over at Elizabeth. "Let's go, Ms. Morris." He stepped out onto the concrete curb. The smell of gasoline wafted up to his nostrils.

Elizabeth followed suit and closed the door behind her. She pulled out a .44 revolver from the front of her pants, flicking the chamber open then closing it.

Roger's eyes fell to the hardware. "A .44. Nice. You know how to handle one of those?"

They slinked into the nearby shadowy alley. "What's that supposed to mean?" Elizabeth asked with a tense voice.

"It means precisely what I asked. That's a beefy piece. I'd hate to see you bonk your own head with the recoil."

"You just focus on you, cowboy. I've been shooting this thing since I was a little girl."

"Then all you had to say was yes."

Elizabeth grumbled under her breath. "You have some nerve to say that to me."

Roger came to the end of the brick wall and peeked around it. He saw another masked figure kneeling at the end, still cloaked in shadows. "We've caught up with your brother at least." He felt a hand on his upper back. He turned his head when he stumbled forward from a push.

Elizabeth's voice came from behind him. "Hurry up then. I don't want to be out here all night."

Daniel turned around at the scuffle. "Be quiet you two." He returned his gaze to the store across the street and pointed forward. "Looks like that's our way in."

"The front door?" Roger asked. "Shouldn't we like go in the side entrance or something?"

Elizabeth's hand snaked around Roger's neck and pinched his ear. "No, idiot. We're trying to cause a fuss, remember? God, get it together already."

"Let's get this done already and head home." Daniel pumped his shotgun. "Everyone ready?"

Roger opened his revolvers' chambers and closed them. "I'm loaded and ready."

"I can feel the dirt on my perfect skin already," Elizabeth whined in a nasally voice. "Yes, for the love of God. Let's go."

Daniel snickered. "Women. Am I right, Rog?"

Elizabeth growled behind Roger.

Daniel shook his head and cleared his throat. "Okay, time for work." He stood up and took off in a mad dash toward the storefront. Roger and Elizabeth followed in lock step behind him.

He crashed through the front doors...

8

Daniel leveled the shotgun at the woman in front of him behind the marble counter. "Keep your hands where I can see them, little lady. If they fall, so do you." His voice escalated into a scream. "That goes for everyone." He looked to his left and saw Ronald Alexander cowering in the corner. "Well, who do we have here?"

Roger leveled his revolvers toward the lady behind the counter as Daniel approached Ronald. "Easy now. Keep those hands where we can see them, and we all go home tonight."

Daniel reached out and pulled Ronald toward him by the collar. "You're the wannabe mayor, aren't you?"

"That's right," Ronald choked out.

Daniel threw him back onto his butt. "Just stay there, Mr. Mayor, and we'll be done in a moment. If you're wondering where your little bodyguard is, he's not coming."

Roger chuckled. "We convinced him to go back and stay in the car. Understand? You're all alone tonight."

Elizabeth pushed past Roger and slammed a plastic bag on the counter. "Fill this."

The woman opened the register in front of her and stuffed the bag with piles of green bills. "I'm sorry, this is all we have," she said through tears now falling down her face.

"You're pathetic," Elizabeth said. "Hurry up, we don't have all night." Her hand shot out and plucked the bag from the crying woman. "We've got it. Let's go already."

"There's just one last thing before we go," Daniel said. He took the butt of the rifle and slammed it into Ronald's abdomen.

Ronald's hands fell to his stomach as he doubled over in pain and wiggled on the ground with groans.

"Why don't you just try and take our guns from our cold dead hands? That's the only way you're getting them."

Ronald sat gasping on the tiled floor. "We will make New York safe again from thugs like you. Mark my words. I'm not afraid of you. None of us are. You're just cowards that hide behind guns and masks."

"Bravo," Daniel said. "That's quite the inspiring speech. I see why you went into politics." He delivered a withering kick into Ronald's stomach. "Don't get too cocky now. Silver tongued devils do not get special treatment from folks like me. You're trying to take away our livelihood." He turned to the cashier, her bottom lip quivering. "Don't you agree? A man has a right to defend himself. Isn't that right? Our safety is not for pustules on America's backside like this bottom feeder to decide." His right foot nudged the groaning politician.

"Who are you?" Ronald asked.

"You know who we are."

Ronald regained his composure, sat up, and looked at the man above him. "You're with the FFC, aren't you?"

"We at the Firearm Freedom Coalition are watching you closely, Mr. Alexander. We're always vigilant. Don't forget."

He backed away, pump action squared at Ronald all the while. "Let's skedaddle."

"Music to my ears," Roger said. He tapped Elizabeth's shoulder. "You first."

"Finally," Elizabeth said. She clutched the bag laying on the counter, passed by Roger, and went out the door.

Daniel and Roger came shoulder to shoulder. Weapons still pointed at the people inside. "Be smart about this," Roger said. "Don't make us come back to teach you another lesson, Mr. Alexander."

Both men backed out of the glass double doors and, once outside, dashed off into the darkness.

Ronald got to his feet and stumbled over to the marble countertop. He leaned against it, coughing as he asked, "Are you alright?"

"Yes, I'm fine." She reached up and wiped her eyes. "I just never thought I'd see the FFC ever do such a thing. I don't understand."

"Don't worry, Miss," Ronald said. "I'll get to the bottom of this. I swear it."

"God bless you, Mr. Alexander," she said with a smile.

———————

Back in the van...

Everyone filed in, Daniel in the front, Roger and Elizabeth in the back. Daniel's hand shot out and poked Bruce's shoulder. "Step on it."

Bruce's foot pressed the pedal, causing the vehicle to begin moving. "How'd it go in there?"

"Everything went according to plan this time. That could

be because all of its participants were accounted for," Daniel snapped.

"I'm never going to live that down, am I?" Bruce asked.

"No. As a matter of fact, I'm going to let Eddy know where his buddy was while he was getting shot. Does that sound better? After all, the best way of getting past something like this is to get it out in the open. Don't you agree?"

"I think you've made your point," Elizabeth said from the back.

"It's not like you're innocent in it either," Daniel fired back. "It's half your fault. The only three doing our jobs that night were me, Rog, and Eddy. That's the cold hard truth of the matter. If father asks, that's what I'll tell him. That's the end of it."

"Of course you would." Elizabeth crossed her arms. "You're training Rog, so why wouldn't you brag on him? It makes you look better." Elizabeth looked over and winked at Roger. "The better he does, the closer you get to an actual command after all."

"I won't deny that, but I will correct you on one thing. If he fucked up, he'd be treated just the same as your ex up here. Thus far, he hasn't given me reason. In fact, so far he's been impressive. He's shown he doesn't screw around, and he watches out for his brothers. Clear enough, Sis?"

"Crystal," she muttered under her breath. She stole a glance at her side and scooted closer to Roger. She leaned close to his ear and whispered. "It seems my brother is quite smitten with you."

Roger's head shot away from the voice and banged into the window. "Ah shit. Don't startle me like that. Please."

Elizabeth erupted into a cackle. "That's hilarious. You're so jumpy. It would almost be cute if it wasn't so pathetic."

Roger narrowed his eyes but kept his mouth shut except for a low growling noise.

"Aw, did I make you mad?"

"At least he said please," Daniel quipped from up front. "How many of your boyfriends have ever used that word?"

"Excuse me, but -" Roger started.

"Shut up," Elizabeth said.

"Okay."

9

"Finally," Bruce said. "Home, sweet home." He threw the van into park and unfastened his seat belt. "I can't wait to get some sleep."

"Which reminds me, I need to get settled in myself," Roger said as he opened the back door. "I just threw all my stuff on the bed and got ready for this."

"You live here now?" Elizabeth followed him out of the car.

"I gave him one of the spare rooms. It seemed the least we could do after his service," Daniel said with a slam of the door. "You want to help him get settled in, Liz?"

Elizabeth scoffed. "As if."

"Tough luck, buddy," Daniel said with a chortle, elbowing Roger's ribs. "Maybe she'll eventually come around."

Elizabeth spat on the asphalt below. "Ugh, men." Her stare lingered on Roger's back as he and her brother made their way to the front door.

Bruce walked past and looked back at her. "What's the matter?"

"None of your business," she said.

He turned around, stepped in front of her, and blocked her progress. "You want him, don't you?"

"What the hell business is it of yours?"

"I didn't hear a no."

"Screw off. How's that for a no?" Her hands fell to her hips. She shifted her weight to the left. "Now get out of my way. I'm going to bed."

"I'm not done talking about us." Bruce reached out and grabbed Elizabeth's hands.

She jerked her hands away. "Get away from me. You wanted out, so we're done. Forever. If you insist on doing this, you'll be explaining it to my brother or father next. Do you understand me?"

Bruce bit his bottom lip. "I understand the princess needs her big bad brother to deal with her problems."

"Piss off. I don't need any of them to handle my affairs. Who I involve myself with is of no concern to you anymore. As I recall, you were the one running and dodging me. You think I will just forget that shit?"

"You don't just handcuff a man and do..." his face turned red, "that to him without his permission. I wasn't ready yet."

"You are now?" Her thin mouth curled upward. "I can arrange that if you really want to."

Beads of sweat rolled down the sides of Bruce's brow. "Stop deflecting already and have a real conversation."

The door opened to reveal Roger leaning his head outside. "Everything alright out here?"

"What are you doing here?" Bruce asked without turning around to face Roger.

"Daniel tasked me with seeing what was taking you two so long out here."

Elizabeth shoved her way past Bruce and slithered up

beside Roger. She leaned up on her tip toes and whispered in his ear. "Everything's fine now that you're here. Shall I show you to your room?" her breathy voice asked.

Roger stuttered. "If you wish, Ms. Morris. I don't want to keep you up too long."

"How considerate." She looked back at Bruce and gave a wide smile. Her eyes zoomed back and traced Roger's chiseled, rugged jaw line. "I don't mind getting to sleep late. Let me show you. Come." She clutched his hand and dragged him inside, leaving Bruce outside alone with the chorus of crickets.

Inside Roger's room...

"I swear, you'd think we were in high school with the way they carried on downstairs." Elizabeth twisted the knob open with her free hand. She pushed the door and pulled Roger inside. Her eyebrows raised. "Oh wow, you only have two bags?"

"I was forced to leave in a hurry."

"At least Danny set you up in a good room." Elizabeth surveyed the room. A twin-sized bed sat to their left with a small window behind it. A television sat perched across from it, on top of a dresser. Her gaze turned further right. "I see he even got you a room with an adjoining bath." She turned to look at him. "I'm jealous."

"I imagined you had the best room in the place. Honestly, I just said I'd like something with a window, and he gave me this," Roger said with his free hand scratching his neck.

Elizabeth smiled and moved to within a foot. She looked up at him. "Now, why would you think that?"

"Your father seems to be a man who doesn't skimp when it comes to accommodations for him and his family." He wrapped her hands in his and squeezed her hands with gentle strength. "Especially when it comes to his gorgeous daughter."

Elizabeth backed up a step and removed her hands from his grasp. "Easy there, stud. Don't get ahead of yourself and start believing those idiots that were joking with you about me."

Roger tilted his head. "You mean you're not -"

Her focus became her shoe tops. "No." She looked back up at him. "I mean, maybe."

Roger chuckled and moved to sit at the head of the bed.

"Did I say something funny?"

"Not at all. I just didn't expect that reaction from you, Miss Morris. You always seem to be so controlled and to know exactly what you want is all."

Elizabeth stomped over and sat on the other side of the bed. "What would you know? You just got here a few days ago."

"You're right." His leg kicked out. He fell back onto the bed, staring up at the ceiling "It was just the impression I received when I first saw you."

"Really?" Elizabeth asked. "You got all that from our first conversation?"

"I'll be honest. A half-naked Bruce sprinting toward me was probably the most iconic image I remember about that meeting. That and him asking for my drawers. That was memorable."

She scooted closer. "So, you did see him back then? You lied to me?"

"Guilty as charged. Do you know why? A lot of women scoff when we men try and explain it."

Elizabeth planted her right hand onto the bed and leaned toward Roger. "I'm sure it'll be worth a laugh. Why?"

"We men are trained from a young age to help other guys when it comes to women troubles. Even if we have no idea who they are. We see a kindred spirit. After all, one day we may be the ones needing help. Does that make sense? I assumed ladies had a similar code."

"That's an elegant way of saying 'Bros before hoes'," Elizabeth giggled.

His head rolled to the side and his eyes fell on her. "You also have to keep in mind that I wanted to prove myself to the boys. Surely you can understand?"

"As deluded as your boyish intentions were..." she trailed off. "I understand. You chose poorly there, but I suppose I can forgive such a naïve action just this once. Just don't lie to me again. Got it, Mr. Johnson?"

"Of course, Ms. Morris. You can call me Roger." He sat up with a beaming smile.

She stood up and moved toward the door. She stopped in front of it and turned back to him. "If you must, you can call me Elizabeth. Now, if you'll excuse me, I'm going to go to bed."

"Good night, Elizabeth."

"Good night, Roger." She exited the room and closed it behind her.

She looked to her left and saw Daniel with his hand up coming down the hallway. "What are you doing here? This is Rog's room." His eyes moved to the door and back to his sister. "Oh, I get it."

"You understand nothing," Elizabeth said.

"You don't like the new guy?"

Elizabeth left a lingering gaze at the door before directing her eyes back to her brother. "There's something different about him. I can't quite put my finger on it."

"He said no, huh? Don't worry. There're loads of fish in the sea that like it when a lady -"

Elizabeth raised a lone index finger. "Shut the fuck up. That's not what I meant, and you know it. He didn't even try."

"Try?" Daniel asked. He shoved his hands into his pocket.

"Yeah, to get physical. You know what I mean."

"You mean like with Bruce? Yeah. He seems like a different kind of guy."

Elizabeth rubbed her arm and looked away. "You might want to talk to Bruce."

"Why?"

She turned back to her brother. "He's getting pushier ever since we broke up. I'm just lucky you sent Rog outside to break it up when you did."

Daniel jerked his hands out of his pockets and cracked his knuckles. "I never sent Rog. If I knew it was happening, I'd have kicked his ass."

"You didn't..." She looked back at the door. "Huh, weird."

"Come on," Daniel said, guiding Elizabeth down the corridor. "Let's go pay Bruce a little visit, shall we? Now what did he do exactly?"

"He grabbed my shoulders and began..."

10

"What happened to you?" Eddy asked. A constant beeping permeated the room. He watched Bruce standing at the foot of the bed. "You look like you went up against a six-hundred-pound gorilla in a fistfight."

"He wouldn't tell me either. He was fine last night when we got back," Roger said from the chair beside the bed.

"It's nothing at all," Bruce said. "Danny was just a little mad at me."

"A little?" Eddy asked with a laugh and a groan. "Ooh, don't make me laugh. You must have really pissed him off. What did you do?"

Bruce raised a hand, clutching an ice pack to his darkening eye. "It's personal."

"It's about his sister. I can tell already," Eddy said without pause. "Are you still screwing around with her? I thought you wanted out?" His left hand tapped the back of Roger's hand. "Word to the wise. If you do get involved with her, be nice. It sounds obvious, but she has two of the most powerful men at her beck and call. Our friend over there found out firsthand it appears. He's just lucky he's still sucking air after they were done with him."

"Forgetting me," Bruce started, leaning against the foot board, "how have you been doing?"

"Sawbones said I'd be just fine. He said I'm lucky it went in and out. He also said I'm lucky I didn't bleed out entirely." He looked up at Roger at his side. "I guess I've got you to thank for that."

"You don't need to thank me. I just did what came natural at the time."

"I am thanking you anyway. Not a lot of men would do that. You ever need anything, you come to me. I'll get it for you free of charge."

Bruce's eyes snapped open wide. "No charge?"

"You heard me right," Eddy said with a yawn. "Now both of you go get ready for your next assignment. I'll be back in action before you know it."

"You're just waiting for the next sponge bath from the nurse stand-in, aren't you?" Bruce asked with a lascivious grin.

"I can't help it if Ana looks so good in that dress. Can I? Now get going. She'll be here any minute."

Roger smiled and shook his head before standing up. "Take it easy, brother."

"You know it. Oh, one last thing before you go." His left hand shot out and grabbed Roger's wrist. "Keep Daniel safe, won't you? I'm normally the one keeping him in line. I'm giving you that job now. He's hot headed and can get himself in trouble. Back him up the same way you did me. Got it?"

"I'll do everything I can. Don't you worry. Just relax and get better."

"Good. Now get out." A knock at the door interrupted him. "My bath is ready, gentlemen."

Roger and Bruce made for the door and opened it to show a woman in a short skirt, a sponge, and a large bucket filled with water. Bruce shoved his way past her.

She glared at the man, her mouth muttering something incoherent under her breath. She looked back at Roger and moved out of the way.

"After you." He gestured inside.

"Thanks, handsome." She slinked past him into the room. He closed the door and paced down the corridor. He sniffed, reached into his pants pocket, and took out a tissue. He dabbed under his nose and shoved it back into his pocket. "I must be getting a cold or something. That's just my luck."

8PM...

Daniel sat in the leather-bound chair and leaned back, his feet resting against the mahogany desk. "Any word on how the mayoral campaign is going?"

Bernard opened the stainless-steel lighter and flicked the wheel. A flame roared to life and engulfed the bulbous brown cigar. White smoke flowed out of his mouth. "The last debate's coming up tonight. We'll see how you've done so far."

Daniel waved his hand back and forth, fanning in front of him. He looked above his father, out of the enormous paneled windows. "We did everything he asked and more. He'll have his talking points and events to point to. It's just as we agreed."

"That remains to be seen." Bernard took the stogie out of his mouth, reached down to the shot glass full of amber, and upended it. "Regardless, I have something for you to do tonight to cement our end of the deal."

Daniel leaned forward. "Whatever it is, consider it done already."

"Slow down, boy. Remember what I told you. Carefully consider the job. If you jump in without looking, that's when men die unnecessarily." He grunted, and the end of the cigar glowed red. A cloud of smoke escaped the corner of his mouth. "Still, I guess you should be fine. I need you and a small group to go to this address." He pointed to a lone piece of paper displayed on his desk. "That'll point you to Whitney Garrisan's abode."

Daniel looked up and scratched the side of his head. "Who is this guy exactly?"

"She's the campaign advisor to Ronald's opponent. I want you to go over there and make sure she gets shaken up. Don't let her know who you are for the love of God, boy. It's just a simple B & E. Tie her to a chair and convince her to give some bad advice. You know?"

"Maybe her piece on the side will finally catch up to her?"

"You do know she's married?" Bernard asked.

"Exactly. The rumor is she's cheating on her husband with the landscaper they hired. Don't you keep up on gossip with these rich types?"

"I keep up with who I need to. Don't try and overextend yourself. That's the first rule in this life. Never forget that. If you take on too much, you make mistakes." He snuffed out the brown cylinder in the nearby ash tray. "And for the love of God, learn how to set up a crossfire. You're damned lucky, from what I heard, that you didn't end up with friendly fire. You're going to get someone killed with amateur hour shit like that. Just look at your friend. Do you realize it was your fault he was nearly killed?"

Daniel looked off to the side, his voice softer. "I didn't order him to go out there."

"When you have men under your command, you're responsible for them. That's the first rule of leadership. Have you learned nothing?" Bernard sighed, turning in place with a squeak of his chair. "You sent him around the back. You shot through the front. Do you not see the problem here? That was stupid. If it wasn't for our newest member, he'd be dead."

"Speaking of, he's working out better than I expected."

"Just don't take your eyes off him. He's new. You can't expect the world."

"Worried about the rumors of Liz being interested in him?" Daniel kicked back with a smug smile.

Bernard slammed a fist into the desk. "What now? I thought she was with that ignoramus friend of yours? Bruce, was it?"

Daniel's right hand clenched in his lap. "Yeah. They're not together anymore after what he did."

"What did he do to my little girl?"

"I took care of it, Dad. He won't bother her anymore. I can guarantee that personally."

Bernard stood up. "You'd better be right." He picked up the coat that was draped around his chair and tried to put it on. "If I find out he's hurt my girl, I'll bury him myself. I hate to lose manpower, but a man has to have priorities. Right, Son?"

Daniel jumped out of the seat and moved to help his father into the jacket. "That's right. Otherwise, we're no better than animals."

"At least you've been listening a little," he grunted. "I

have a business meeting to attend to. Gather a few of the boys and get the car ready before you start preparing for your little adventure tonight. I'm going to go and start working on the other end."

"Other end?" Daniel asked, helping his father's second arm into the jacket.

"I'm going to a sit down with our firearm suppliers and secure us a pipeline. Someone has to secure the future of the family if this doesn't pan out."

"On it, but don't worry, Father. It'll work out just fine."

"We'll see." Bernard walked side by side with his son out of the giant double doors.

---

10 PM outside Garrisan's home...

"Does everyone have their gloves on and mask handy?"

"Obviously," Roger's sarcasm laden voice said.

"We're roughing up the campaign manager?" Elizabeth asked, sliding the gray mask over her head.

Daniel reached up and turned the emergency light on. "That was Dad's orders." Daniel brought the serrated knife up to the light above, inspected it, and sheathed it at his side.

"We need a knife for that?" Roger asked. He reached up and turned the light off, cloaking them back into darkness.

"She may not be as cooperative as we'd like. I'm just bringing all the tools to accomplish our goal if she's stubborn." He pulled the thin fabric over his face.

"Good Lord." Roger brought a hand to his forehead and wiped the sweat away before putting on the mask.

"What's wrong with you?" Bruce asked from his right. "You look like you have a fever."

"I feel like crap too," Roger said with a snort.

"You probably caught the cold that dumbass brought in a week ago." Elizabeth leaned forward and stared across Roger after she'd donned her mask.

"It wasn't me," Bruce fired back. "I've been fine for the past few days."

Daniel turned in place and faced the back of the van. "Quiet," Daniel said, his voice full of steel. "Now as I understand it, Ms. Garrisan owns a security system. Any ideas how we're going to nullify it?"

"Is this one of those systems that's connected to the local PD or just makes a lot of noise?" Roger asked.

"I have no idea," Daniel said. "Just assume it's connected to be safe. Can you disarm it?"

"In theory."

"What the hell does that mean?" Elizabeth asked from his side.

"I mean I've never had to, but I did learn how to from Tanya when I first joined. We're also redirecting any calls for help to this laptop." He patted the laptop on his lap. "My little scouting trip earlier wasn't for show. I messed with their phone line while I was at it."

"You know Tawnie?" Elizabeth asked. "If she likes you well enough, you can't be all bad." She directed her attention to her brother in the front. "I vote we let Rog try."

"Seriously?" Bruce asked. "He just said he's not sure."

"Tanya is the best there is. If she taught him, I trust he can do it." Elizabeth looked out the nearby window.

"A rare vote of confidence from my sister. Kid, you must be something." Daniel twisted the key and removed it from the ignition. "How long do you need?"

"I'd say give me ten minutes. I'll need a lookout in case she gets curious."

"I'll go with him," Daniel said. "I've been waiting for a chance to scope the place out anyway. You two play nice while we're gone." He gave a pointed glare at Bruce who turned away. "Or do you need another lesson in common decency?"

"I'm going with you." Elizabeth started to open the door. "I'm not staying behind with him."

"I'm fine with watching the car." Bruce gazed out of the opposite window.

"Yes, I'm sure you are." Daniel glared at him. He turned his head and looked at Elizabeth. "Just stay quiet, and I don't care. We ready?"

"I sincerely hope we have a toolbox in the back." Roger got onto his knees and peeked over the seats. "Ah, good. With this I should be fine." He grunted and leaned down. A metallic clunking pierced the cabin as he lifted the box and sat it on his lap. He opened it and dug through.

"I guess it's a good idea that I insisted on taking the van. Wait, you're going through that now?" Daniel asked.

"It'd be a lot quieter to not have tons of steel tools shifting around a metal container." He plucked a pair of wire cutters and a screwdriver out and shoved them into his pants pocket. "There, that'll be much quieter."

Elizabeth and Daniel pushed open their doors and exited. Roger scooted over and followed suit.

Elizabeth held the door open and shut it behind him. "Don't get used to this, Mr. Johnson. I'm not just some common door-girl after all."

"Oh, perish the thought."

Daniel pointed at the house. "If you two are done flirting, let's go."

"Alright, here's the plan." Roger pointed to the fence surrounding the two-story house. "We're jumping the fence and heading around the back."

"Why the back?" Daniel asked.

"The models I trained against had to be fed power from somewhere. This normally came from a pseudo fuse box of sorts outside. Generally, that's where they put the power boxes they install on the house. They don't put it out front since they're an eyesore. Now I didn't see one earlier, but I didn't get a good look in the backyard."

"They don't put it inside the house?" Elizabeth asked, bringing her hand up to her mouth and stifling a snicker. "I wonder if they realize the criminals come from outside?"

"Would you want a box the size of a large three ring binder jutting out in some hallway?" Roger asked. "Because I sure wouldn't."

"Point taken."

"Let's go. Look for a back door to that fence. I don't fancy climbing that tall wooden monstrosity," Daniel said with a step forward across the black pavement.

The group reached the fence and the sound of crunching grass filled the balmy night air. Daniel led the group then stopped without warning, causing Roger to bump into him from behind. "Back off. Give me some room." The quiet sound of the gate squeaking accompanied his voice. "I found the gate." He swung the entrance open and filed inside. "Make sure to close it behind you."

"Duh," Elizabeth said. She glided the gate closed.

"She's still awake," Roger whispered. "Stay low and behind me." He passed Daniel, hunched over as he crept forward.

The house's two visible windows had their curtains closed. A small automatic light sprang to life as he passed by. "Shit," Roger muttered. He took off and jumped into the bushes lining the house. He beckoned them over. "Hurry up."

The twins looked at each other, shrugged, and hurled themselves into place on either side of him. Elizabeth growled into his ear. "What the fuck are we doing?"

Roger raised a hand and placed it over her mouth. "Stay quiet and get down." He ducked down below the shrubbery at the sound of a lock clicking.

The back door, a few feet away, opened. A lanky older man in glasses stepped outside and stood there for a few seconds. "Damned raccoons are always setting it off. It's just a waste of power is all it is. Why we ever wasted the money for it is beyond me, but she just had to have it." He stepped back inside and shut the door.

Roger removed his hand from Elizabeth's mouth and let out a sigh of relief. "Believe it or not, this is good news."

"How do you figure?" Daniel asked at his side. He pushed a stray twig away from his face. "You suck at finding hiding places by the way. What do you think, Liz?"

Elizabeth brought a finger to her lips and held it there, staring into the backyard. "What? I think gagging me physically wasn't necessary."

Roger stood up and brushed his jeans off. "Sorry about that. Can't take any chances." He looked over to the back door. "Oh dear. Well, let's hope I'm right."

"What? What's wrong?" Daniel asked, approaching from his side. He spit on the grass below.

"They have a newer model with the power box inside. Now, normally these setups have the user interface just inside the door. However, I don't believe they've actually armed their system yet."

"How on God's green earth would you know that?" Elizabeth asked, still dusting off her jeans.

"He opened the door without a siren going off, didn't he?" Roger asked.

"Couldn't he have just set the alarm after he went back inside?" Daniel asked.

Roger shrugged. "Maybe, but the good news is, if the alarm goes off it doesn't take long for me to shut it down. I'd need a couple of minutes at most. Police wouldn't get called unless it's on for a prolonged period."

"This is starting to look dicey, Danny. We may want to call it quits. I'm sure Daddy would understand."

"We're not leaving without finishing the job, and that's that." Daniel turned to Roger. "Can you do it?"

"Absolutely. The components inside the keypad are universal. The hardest part is simply getting the front off, which takes a minute or two."

"Then we're going." Daniel removed the pistol from his belt line and held it at the ready. He moved to the right of the door and hunched down. "Liz, we're on the personnel. Rog, you're only focusing on the alarm."

Roger reached into his pants pocket and retrieved his tools. He crept beside Daniel and nodded.

Elizabeth lined up behind Roger and patted his shoulder. "Move aside." She rubbed against him as she moved in front of the door and him. She turned back, licked her ruby lips, and smirked. "Watch where you're looking." She returned her attention to the door and unholstered her .44. "I'll go left, you go right?"

"That's as good a system as any I suppose," Daniel said. "Do you have the tape handy?"

"I've got something better than tape. How do handcuffs sound?"

Daniel rolled his eyes. "Tell me you're not serious. Stick to the damned plan."

Elizabeth's free hand reached inside her coat pocket and removed a roll of tape. "Here it is, you big baby. You're too serious. Of course I'd bring the tape." She stashed the roll in her pocket.

"You just carry around metal cuffs?" Roger asked, mouth agape.

"A girl's got to be prepared." She turned back and tilted her head to the side. "Why? Does that make you nervous?"

"It should." Daniel reached out and squeezed the knob. He twisted it and whispered. "We go in quiet on three. We'll immobilize them and tape their mouths. I'll take care of the husband, and Lizzie questions Ms. Garrisan herself." He held up his other hand and raised a finger with every count. "One, two, three, go." He nudged the door open with his shoulder and turned the corner.

11

Daniel crept down the carpeted hallway. A familiar nasally male voice came from the room in front of him. "Whitney, honey, you need your rest. Come to bed, won't you?"

"I can't. I don't have time," a female voice said. "I have to make calls to the convention center to set up our next speech after tonight's abysmal failure. That's not even mentioning the fact that I'm on the hook for distancing Mr. Herschel from the FFC. He can't be within a million miles of this. After that, we'll pull those records of his membership and erase the log of the whole thing happening. I do not have time right now. I have too many phone calls to make, sweetie."

Footsteps thudded through the house. "At least promise me you'll sleep at some point tonight. Okay?"

Daniel halted when he came to the edge of the room and leaned against the wall. He peeked around the corner and saw a kitchen. Whitney sat at the lone table beside a discarded phone, papers scattered everywhere. The man had his hand on her shoulder. He ducked back behind cover.

"Alright. Don't forget to set the alarm before you come up." More footsteps came from the kitchen until they became fainter.

"Hmm?" Whitney asked. "I thought you went to bed?" She paused, her voice becoming shrill. "Who are you? Get out of my house! Bernie, call 911. There's a crazy in here."

"Son of a bitch," Daniel said to himself as he stepped out from cover and marched into the kitchen. He saw Whitney backing up toward him away from Elizabeth, who sheathed her revolver. She pulled out the roll of tape and ripped off a piece.

Daniel wrapped his arms around Whitney and held her in place.

His sister laughed and stuck the tape over her mouth. "Quiet now, Ms. Garrisan. Your husband's in bed now, isn't he?" She reached into her back jeans pocket and twirled a pair of cuffs around her index finger until she caught it and opened them. Her hand darted forward and clasped one end around Whitney's wrist.

Daniel pushed her down into the seat and attached the other end between the chair slats and to her other wrist behind her. "I'll go attend to your husband now." He stood up and made for the stairs.

"You'll need this." Elizabeth tossed him another pair of restraints and a knife from the nearby knife rack..

He caught them and continued upstairs.

Whitney yanked against the restraints.

Elizabeth ripped the tape from her mouth. "What is it, dear? Decide to make my job easy?"

"You can't do this to me? Do you have any idea who I

work for? You're finished. They'll throw you in a hole for the rest of your life for this."

Elizabeth ducked down and looked at her dead on. "Honey, trust me when I say you're not in the position to make threats. You have no idea who we are, but we know everything about you. Information can be just as deadly as a bullet with the right usage. I urge you to listen to us and then make your decision." She stood up and opened various drawers. She stopped at the third. "Ooh, what do we have here?" She reached in and removed a large knife. "This could be useful if you decide to be stubborn."

"You wouldn't dare."

Elizabeth dropped it back in with a clatter and closed it with her hip. "Maybe you're right. It'd leave too many marks for you to go cry to the media. Your situation is unique. I'll need to get creative."

Roger entered the room. He walked to the large table and leaned against it, arms folded in front of him. "The alarm's as good as gone. They couldn't set it off, even if they wanted to."

"Who the hell are you?" Whitney asked.

Roger watched Elizabeth rifle through the wooden drawers. "I'm their fairy godfather, couldn't you tell?"

"You put them up to this?"

Roger's head leaned back, and he let loose a boisterous laugh. "Me?"

"What have we here?" Elizabeth asked. She hefted a large bag of apples over her shoulder. "This will do."

"You're going to eat my fruit?"

"R, why don't you go and see how D is doing? I'll take care of this."

"Sure." He kicked off from the table and made his way up the stairs.

He heard Elizabeth's voice fade as he ascended. "Bruises can be explained away easily. Maybe your husband found out about your little affair and went off the deep end. It's always the quiet ones after all."

Roger traced the railing with his gloved left hand as he climbed. He saw an open doorway in front of him with Daniel standing over a restrained man in bed. "Alarm's taken care of, along with Ms. Garrisan. Need any help up here?" He closed the door behind him.

Daniel's gaze was still locked on the terrified man's wide eyes. "I'm good. Take a seat and learn something. I'll show you how to extract information."

Roger saw a lone chair in the corner to his left and took a seat. "I thought torture was unreliable when it comes to intel?"

"That old myth? I'll tell you what I know." He extracted his knife, brought it up to his mouth and licked the blade, never looking away from his victim. "You give a man enough fear, and he'll crack. I guarantee it. The problem is when they lie to get out of it. I have a system for that." He sat next to the man chained to the bed and put the knife in his view. "See, most men love playing the hero. They want to feel like they gave 'the bad guy' his comeuppance and saved their woman. Right?"

"I'm with you so far," Roger said.

"What they almost always fail to realize is that most of us in the information industry don't care. We don't care if they're the ones beneath our gaze or their oh so adorable loved ones. If they lie, we go after them."

"That works?"

"Would you lie to the man holding a literal knife to your family's throat?"

"If I had assurances they wouldn't be harmed, probably

not."

Daniel gently dragged the knife across Bernie's throat. "That's cause you're a smart man. Most, in my experience, aren't. They seem to think we're animals or something and refuse to even have civil discourse. It's like they think insulting me is a grand idea or something."

"It's a mystery why," Roger said in a deadpan voice.

"Indeed." His voice grew steely. He leaned forward, spit landing on Bernie's face as he spoke. "Are you going to be smart or an idiot?"

Bernie shivered in place, eyes never leaving Daniel. He shook his head.

"What the hell does that mean?" Roger asked.

"It means," Daniel's free hand reached down and grabbed Bernie's crotch, "that he's a pussy that won't answer. What say you? Answer, or you're going to be a soprano right quick."

Bernie continued shaking his head. "I won't be dumb. No, sir. Please don't hurt me."

Daniel released his hold and smirked. "Good boy. The next time I won't be quite so gentle, so answer on time please. Let's keep it civilized after all."

"Yeah." Roger stood up and moved to the windows, peering outside. "We're not savages or something."

"I have to apologize for my friend here. He's new. He meant to say, we're not savages unless your wife makes us be. You kind of get the raw deal here, dude. I almost feel bad for you, honestly. There's no real way for you to stop this if she doesn't comply."

"C-comply?" Bernie stuttered. "What do you want her to do?"

"Take a wild guess, numb nuts."

"Throw the race? She'll never do that."

Daniel jammed the knife against Bernie's throat. "Which is where you'll come in. If she's stubborn, we're bringing her in here to see what happens. Hopefully you'll be able to convince her to change her mind." He looked over his shoulder at Roger. "Go see how our girl's doing, won't you? Bring her up in a few minutes if she's being difficult. I have just the thing to change her mind."

Roger hopped up. "Sure. It sounds like it could be a long night." He exited and slammed the door closed behind him. He descended the stairs at a sluggish pace and turned the corner. Elizabeth was staring at Whitney dead in the eye, the bag of apples hanging at her side.

"Nothing to say yet? No matter, those bruises are just the beginning. You can make this end at any time if you just say the magic words."

Whitney spat. A darkened patch appeared on Elizabeth's shirt.

Elizabeth reared back and slammed the bag of produce against Whitney's rib cage. "Defiant I see." She inspected the dark spot on her top. "Good for you."

"Not so good for old Bernie though," Roger said. "Our resident specialist is having his way with him. The longer you hold out, the more he suffers. You may want to tell the nicer of the two here," he jabbed a thumb toward Elizabeth, "so we can get out of your hair sooner."

"He doesn't know anything. He has nothing you want." Whitney's hand was opening and closing behind her. "Leave him alone."

Elizabeth dropped the bag and moved to Roger. She wrapped an arm around his shoulders. "We'd be happy to." She leaned her head into his neck. "All we ask in return is that you accidentally release a few bad press releases that damage Mr. Herschel."

"Say, for example, his affiliation with the FFC," Roger said.

Elizabeth brought a finger up to her chin. "Or maybe he killed someone in a drunk driving incident and they hushed it up? I mean the voters have a right to know these things."

"You want me to sell out the future mayor? Who do you think you are?"

Roger took a step forward. "Who we are is of no importance to one such as you. We're merely the arbiters of truth is all." He circled around behind Whitney. He motioned Elizabeth over with a flick of his finger. "We have a little something to show you upstairs. Your husband has something he'd like to say to you. Don't try anything." He grabbed both of her arms and gripped them tightly.

Elizabeth slid the key into the lock and twisted. The lock opened with a click and the cuffs fell open. In one motion she slid them off and linked her other wrist into the bindings so that both hands were confined behind her.

"Stand," Roger said.

Whitney stood up, Elizabeth on one side, Roger on the other. The three marched toward the stairs. "You don't want to do this. Please, no." Her bottom lip quivered. "Surely one of you has a conscience."

"Don't look at me, honey," Elizabeth said with a shove into her back, causing Whitney to stumble forward. "Now get up there. Your husband has something to show you."

The group climbed the stairs and opened the door. Whitney exhaled and fell to her knees. "Don't do this."

Roger leaned down and squeezed her arm. "Watch. You need to see what stubbornness gets him."

Elizabeth squatted down and used her arms to force Whitney's head back toward the display.

Daniel held his knife at his side. Blood dripped onto the

floor. "Looks like the audience is here. Ready? Blame your wife or God for this." He placed the cold steel against Bernie's chest and traced down his body, leaving a thin red trail as it went. The body underneath bucked against the restraints as he hovered over his nether regions. His grunting became incessant and loud.

Daniel used his free hand to push his head back onto the pillow. "Shut up and be a man about this. You married her. Take responsibility."

"You're killing him!" Whitney lurched forward, tears flowing down her face. "Please, no."

"Killing him?" Roger asked, looking up at the man twitching on the bed, his eyes wide, thrashing against the restraint. He dashed forward and placed two fingers on Bernie's neck and paused. "His heartbeat's off the charts. He's liable to have a heart attack if this keeps up. That is, if he's not already having one. I'm no doctor."

"What kind of weakling are you? I haven't even started yet." He took Roger's old place beside Elizabeth and Whitney. Taking her arm, he dragged her up into a standing position. He pointed at her husband's flailing body with his knife. "This can stop anytime you're ready, sweet cheeks."

"Fuck you," she whispered through tears.

"Finally," Daniel guffawed. "Someone with some sack in this house. How ironic it is that the wife is the one to show it." He leaned down and locked eyes with her, unblinking. "I like that." He straightened up and sidled back to the bed, twirling his knife as he went.

"What do you want me to do?" Whitney asked, her head hanging down, her voice weak. "Just stop this already, you monsters."

Daniel sat down beside Bernie and Roger. "Now you're

beginning to ask the right questions. Good, we've made progress."

Elizabeth stood up behind her and kicked her down to the ground. "We want you to spread a few rumors is all. Leak a few stories to the press. You know how the game's played. Let it be known your benefactor, Mr. Herschel, is a huge proponent of the FFC. He also was the mastermind behind the attack on Mr. Alexander at Thurgooden's."

Whitney looked away and bit her lip.

Daniel scraped his implement further south, followed by muffled howls from Bernie. "I'd hurry up if I loved my husband."

Bernie's back arched off the bed with a stifled scream. Without warning his body went limp and fell back to the bed.

"Oh, God damn," Roger said. He placed his gloved fingers against Bernie's carotid artery. He turned back to the group and shook his head. "The pulse is gone. He must have had a weak heart or something."

Daniel swiped the knife, blood staining the carpet below. His gloved hand wiped off the remaining sticky remnants. "This just got a whole lot worse for somebody. Care to guess who, madam?"

Whitney crumpled onto the floor and released a constant whining that soon turned into wracked sobs. Her shoulders heaved with every wheeze. She looked up at Daniel, snot dribbling out of her nose. She snorted, took a deep breath, and sat up. "I'm not telling you shit." Her hands shook. "Why would I? I'm next, right?"

Daniel held the knife up in front of her. He peered down his nose at her. "There are two ways this can go down. Either do what we say, or you are going to prison for 20 years, give or take."

"That's if the judge likes you," Elizabeth chimed. "If not, you might be looking at slop and beans for the rest of your life. You ever been inside?"

"No." Whitney heaved a breath out.

"Me either. There's a big difference between us though. You know what that is?"

Whitney stared at her husband's body, not responding.

"By the time we're done, there will be no evidence that we were ever here. The knife my associate has is the murder weapon, which presumably has your fingerprints on it. If you'll notice, dear, he has gloves on. If we consider your bruises, I'm afraid that looks like evidence of deviant play. Wouldn't you say, guys?"

Roger planted his hands onto his hips and heaved himself up. "It does look like it. At best, if they don't prosecute, you're looking at a huge public relations disaster. Can you imagine it in the papers? 'Herschel's campaign manager's husband dead due to rough sex games?'"

Daniel knelt and cupped her jaw. He turned her head to look at him. "The other option is easier though. Your husband went off and disappeared. He took none of his possessions. You don't know what happened, but you simply devoted yourself to work. In exchange for your life, just release those stories. Simple."

"Never."

"If that's what you want, fine. Have fun in the dike lodge the rest of your natural born life." He looked up and pointed over his shoulder. "Untie him and get everything ready. We're cleaning up and moving out."

Whitney unleashed a primal, ear splitting scream as she got to her feet. She tumbled forward into Daniel, knocking him back onto the bed. Her head jutted forward with every chomp of her teeth.

"Get the crazy bitch off me," Daniel said, pushing against the rabid woman on top of him.

Roger and Elizabeth took hold of her shoulders and threw her onto the floor with a thud.

Elizabeth placed a foot on the woman's back and leaned on it. "She doesn't seem to want to go with the plan. Do we have a backup?"

"We could always take her out too, if she wants to be like this." Daniel rubbed his clean-shaven jaw.

"Do you have any idea what that would look like?" Roger asked. "Right after a debate one of the campaign managers and her husband disappears? If we leave her as we agreed, we'll take care of everything in one swift stroke. If we bury her too, everything could unravel, boss."

"Hmm." Daniel's right foot swung out from the bed and smashed into Whitney's head. "He has a point, but you're not willing to play along, are you?"

Whitney didn't respond except for a low constant growling.

"I guess you'll try your luck in the court of public opinion then. Tie her beside her husband and prepare the house. We're out of here."

Elizabeth placed more of her weight onto Whitney's back. "Now you're speaking my language." She reached down and clutched the handcuffs, yanking her into a standing position. She kicked her hamstrings, causing her to stumble onto the bed. "Get over there and enjoy your last time with your husband."

Roger placed his hands on her shoulders and held her in place as Daniel held her feet. Elizabeth removed the cuff from one hand and, with fluid grace, attached it to the bed post. She unlocked Bernie's cuffs and stashed them away.

"Now that looks right." Elizabeth formed a square with

her hands, looking down at the couple. "I can just picture the television angle they'll use for this. We're almost like directors."

Daniel sauntered over to Roger and placed a hand on his shoulder. "Go get ready to prepare the alarm system for our departure. Remember, it must look like we were never here. Is that possible?" He jammed the knife into Whitney's now cuffed hands and backed off.

"I didn't have to snip any lines, so it's simply a matter of reconnecting a line. Sure, it's possible. We'll do it on the way out since it arms the system. Alright?"

"Got it." Daniel turned to look at the two women. "It's time to go."

"Aww," Elizabeth whined. "I was just starting to have fun."

"Clean everything up and meet near the entry point. You have ten minutes."

"Fine," Elizabeth pouted. She leaned down and delivered a shattering slap to Whitney's cheek. "One for the road."

Ten Minutes Later...

"We're ready?" Roger asked the twins on either side of him.

"Everything upstairs is clean. Liz, how about downstairs?" Daniel asked.

"The kitchen's as it was before." Elizabeth's foot tapped the hardwood floor. "No one will know we were here so long as the tech wonder boy here doesn't fuck up."

Roger leaned in close to the rectangular box and twisted the screwdriver. "Just a minute or two and I'll be good."

"Who's calling this one in?" Elizabeth asked.

Daniel whipped out his phone. "I will after we're back in the car."

"Won't they find it a little odd to have an anonymous tip on a private household's bedroom business?" Roger asked as he placed the front cover back on. "There, it's like we were never here. Now just leave quickly." He shoved them toward the door.

"Dude, what the hell?" Daniel asked, stumbling out of the door.

"Talk about rude." Elizabeth regained her composure and stole a glance at Roger.

Roger inched the door closed and let loose a heaving breath. "Sorry about that. It can be a little touchy when I'm rearming the system. Sometimes they don't give you as much time as the model I'm used to. Better safe than sorry"

The group walked side by side out of the wooden gate. "Time to make the call, Bro," Elizabeth said leading the group toward the car.

Daniel pressed three buttons and raised the phone to his ear. "Yes, I'd like to file a complaint. I heard loud screaming, crashing, and I could have sworn I heard a gunshot. Location? 1378 Yosemite Avenue. Yes, I think someone's hurt. You should send someone straight away. Thank you." He immediately hung up. "It's done. Let's get out of here." He threw the phone onto the asphalt, pulled out his sidearm and shot the device, shattering it into pieces beside the car. He bent down and collected almost all the pieces, leaving only a few.

"If only you were as polite to everyone," Elizabeth said, swinging open the back-seat door and climbing inside.

Roger leaned down and picked up the remaining pieces of the phone, shoving them into his coat pockets.

Daniel circled around the car and plopped into the

passenger side. He slammed the door shut and looked to his left. "Holy shit, he's still here. Color me surprised you didn't wander off."

"Piss off," Bruce growled.

"I'd watch it if I were you," Daniel said through gritted teeth. "Now get us out of here."

Daniel reclined his chair as the van shifted into gear. "This went pretty well, considering."

Roger hurried into the car and slammed the door shut. "Not to be a wet blanket here, but I mean is this really okay? Her husband is dead now." He glanced out the window as the van started moving away from the scene of their latest crime.

Elizabeth placed a palm on Roger's knees. "Don't worry. They had no idea who we were. If she starts spouting off about intruders, they'll stick her ass in the psych ward."

"Assuming they don't think she's trying to cover up her own crime," Daniel chimed in from the front. "It's more likely they'll think she's trying to obstruct and cause a huge public stink. Either Herschel's campaign manager killed her husband, is a freak in the sack, or is crazy. We win in any case."

"I can't argue with that." Roger looked out at the passing cityscape to his left. "I guess I just feel kind of bad now."

"Bad idea," Bruce said, turning the wheel. "I'd suggest you get rid of that feeling if you want to retain your sanity."

"On the contrary," Elizabeth's hand rubbed up his thigh. "I think it's cute."

"Remove the hand, Liz." Daniel glared into the rear-view mirror.

She pulled back the offending limb and kicked the seat in front of her. "Yeah sure, dad."

12

"Ha," Bernard laughed. "Did you see this morning's paper, Ana?"

"No, sir." A short, long haired brunette poured steaming brown liquid into the coffee mug on the desk. "What happened?"

"My boy did me proud is what. Look at this." He turned the newspaper revealing the headline - 'Herschel's campaign manager loved her husband to death, literally'. He grabbed the cup and slurped. "It was a little sloppy, but a fine piece of work nonetheless."

"I'm sure he'll be proud to hear that, sir."

"Keep it to yourself. Go and find him, would you? I need to speak to him."

Ana bowed her head and scampered out of the room.

"A heart attack." Bernard shook his head and snapped the paper open. "How did he manage that?"

A knock interrupted him. He kept his face buried in the print. "Come in." He flipped the page.

Daniel stepped through and took a seat. "What is it, Pop?"

"Did you see the debate last night?"

"We were a little busy planning while that happened. Why?"

Bernard placed the paper down on the desk. He grabbed the nearby remote and pressed the red button. The television roared to life. "I recorded it in case you wanted to explain something to me. Here it is."

Ronald Alexander and Red Herschel stood behind separate podiums in a giant gymnasium. The woman sitting at the desk in front of them leaned up to the microphone. "Mr. Alexander, you've been saying that public safety is your number one priority. If elected, how will you make a meaningful difference?"

"Well, Jodie, as you might know, I was attacked and assaulted recently by outlaws."

"Yes, but I'm not talking abou-"

"Jodie, please. I was savagely beaten by masked assailants. If this could happen to me, it could happen to anybody. The FFC is a dangerous institution, full of lunatics. I intend to make the city a safer place by getting rid of the tools of violence. After all, one can't inflict harm without the means to do so. Correct?"

Herschel pounded a fist onto his podium. "That's such a bad argument, and you know it. What about the lawful gun owners who stop untold incidents of crime that the news doesn't report on?"

Jodie raised a palm. "Mr. Herschel, I'm sorry, but it is his turn to speak."

Ronald looked over at the man opposite and pointed at him "It's not so farfetched that Mr. Herschel here annoyed, folks. After all, he's a card-carrying member of the FFC. I plan to enact what I call the 'Prudence Initiative for

Firearms'. In this plan we will make the process harder for criminals to gain access to their deadly arsenal."

"How exactly would that happen?" Jodie asked. "There is concern this initiative would limit Americans' right to bear arms. What do you say to that, Mr. Alexander?"

"It's right leaning propaganda, folks. No one's coming to take your guns. Don't listen to conspiracy theories from crazies on the radio or on the internet. We're just trying to make the streets a safer place for mothers and their children."

"Uh huh," Jodie said. "I'm afraid your time is up, Mr. Alexander." She turned to Red. "How do you feel about this issue, Mr. Herschel?"

Bernard pressed a button and the feed paused. "Did you really beat up Ronald?"

"I thought it'd give him a little more credibility. Besides, who doesn't want to?"

"That's true, and it did give him more ammunition." Bernard's voice became serious. "Just be careful improvising in the future. It can totally fuck you without lube if you don't think it through." His tone became jovial. "I have one more thing before you go." Bernard stood up and paced behind his desk. "We might have a problem with last night, boy."

"We fixed it so she'd look nutso. Is she rambling about the mythical criminals that the evidence doesn't support?"

"Indeed she is. There's just one problem. Herschel's endorsing her, saying she'd never lie. It gives credence to her claims. There are rumors swirling around that someone was sent to quiet her. Do you realize what that means?" Bernard stopped pacing and leaned forward on the desk. "If Ronald is suspected, it won't be long before they come sniffing around here. That's just what we need, the damned FBI snooping around."

"What are we going to do?" Daniel asked.

"We need to keep the feds off our backs. The only way to do that is to back off and make sure we covered our tracks. You're absolutely sure everything was in order at Garrisan's?"

"We wore gloves, masks, set the alarm back to its default, and cleaned up after ourselves. There's no way they'll suspect us. I made sure of it."

"Then we'll do a little preliminary work to see. Go see your little crush in the computer department. See what she can find out. Have her fix anything she finds. After that, we'll see where we go. For now, damage control is the name of the game."

Daniel jumped to his feet. "Got it. Anything else?"

"Tell that lazy bitch to get me some more coffee. Would you, Son?"

"Right."

Downstairs...

Daniel knocked on the door and heard nothing other than the clacking of keys. He pushed the door open and saw Tanya furiously pounding away at the keyboard. He could hear her muttering as she typed. "How does a person get this stupid? Honestly!"

Daniel cleared his throat. "Having fun?"

She pushed the rolling chair away from the desk and swiveled around causing her blonde hair to swing around. "Oh joy. What is it this time?"

Daniel swaggered forward and leaned down, looking at the monitor. "Are you serious with this shit? Someone's mad a man held open a door for," he paused and squinted at the screen, "her?"

"The crazy bitches give us all a bad name," Tanya said.

"Regardless," Daniel straightened up and peered down at her, "we have another job for you."

Tanya leaned back, placing her hands behind her head. "Let me guess. 'Tawnie, go hack the Russian government'. No, I bet it's the pentagon. Am I close?"

"You're not that far off."

"Oh, mother of God." Tanya's hand went to her forehead. "What is it now?"

"We're on full damage control after our latest op. We need to see if we're on any radars."

Tanya wheeled forward up to the desktop and resumed typing. "You mean local or federal? It's both, isn't it?"

"The order came from on high."

"Just once I want a job where I don't commit multiple felonies. Don't expect quick results. It'll take a day or two."

"Why?" Daniel asked, pushing a mess of wires away with his feet.

"Do you think I can just hack a government institution on the fly? I bounce my signal around the globe about five times, set up proxies, vpn's, brute force the password, and then actually comb through all their files. This is not some 80's movie, no matter how much you may want it to be."

"Yeah, movie hacking does seem flashier than you make it out to be. They bang on their keyboards, the camera pans into flashing green numbers, and then the password appears out of thin air."

"Welcome back to reality," Tanya sighed. "At least send Rog if you want it done faster. He can help me set this up. He was always good at setting up proper bot nets."

"Rog? You call him Rog?"

Tanya peeked over her shoulder. "So? What about it? Are you jealous or something?"

Daniel turned his back to her. "As if."

"Tell him I'll leave my window open."

Daniel pivoted around. "You'll what?"

Tanya swiveled around with a squeak of her chair. "You heard me. It's a little inside joke we have from way back. Don't get your panties in a bunch."

"What does that even mean?"

Tanya's legs fell open and snapped shut. "I dunno. Why don't you ask him?" She covered her mouth and laughed.

"I'll do just that," he said, storming out of the room.

A high-pitched squeal came from Tanya's chair as she rolled back to the desk. "I might have overdone it a little."

Roger's room...

Roger sat at his desk, a glass jar filled with green buds beside him. He stuffed a sizable portion of the ground up plant matter onto the paper and rolled it up. He brought the joint up to his mouth and licked the side, admiring his handiwork. "Perfect." He shoved it into his pocket and the glass jar into a desk drawer when he heard a knock at his door. He grabbed a nearby spray bottle and gave a long spray into the room. "Come in."

The door opened, and Daniel came in, shutting the door behind him. He fell onto the bed and placed his hands behind his head. "Enjoying the digs I picked out?"

"Of course, sir," Roger said. He pushed himself out of the chair and turned to the bed. "Everything alright?"

"You don't ever have to ask me that, kid. I just came here to ask you a few questions."

"Sure." Roger sat beside Daniel. "What is it?"

"First things first. We need you to go back down to the computer room and help Tanya with something about a bot net. She said you'd know what that meant."

"Yes, it wouldn't be the first time."

"You two are old friends, aren't you?" Daniel asked.

"Yeah."

"What did she mean when she said her window's open for you then?"

Roger's eyes went wide and his cheeks burned. "I think that was just her sense of humor."

"Hmm," Daniel grunted. He sniffed the air. "That pretty much confirms it. You're smoking in here. Don't lie to me. I can smell it. That's what she meant, wasn't it?"

"Please don't tell anyone." Roger looked down at the carpet.

Daniel looked away. "Don't give me that look. Besides, what am I going to do? Go to my father and say 'Hey, Dad, remember that new guy I've been talking up and my future depends on? He loves getting stoned.'? Get real. Like I said, so long as it doesn't interfere, I don't give a shit what you do with your own body." He sat up and turned his focus back to Roger. "Don't you make me regret that."

"You've been talking me up?"

"That's not what's important right now," Daniel said. "The other thing I'm here about is my sister. Do I need to say it?"

"To be frank, I'm not exactly the only advancing party, sir." Roger raised his hands up in a surrendering gesture.

"I know, and call me Daniel. It gets stuffy hearing sir all the time." He stood up and moved to the window, peering out over the tree line. "Everybody loves joking around about her crushes. The unwritten rule here is to stay away from her, or go all in. You don't fuck with her feelings." He turned around and pointed at Roger. "Unfortunately for you, she seems to have taken an interest in you. Now I'm not going to go psycho big brother and threaten you or anything if you date her."

"Oh good."

"I will, however, warn you not to mess with her. Either tell her you're not interested or give it a go. That's all. I'm not her keeper, but I will not suffer a guy just trying to get his dick wet in my sister and then dumping her like a used condom." He took a step forward and his voice grew lower. "Understand me?"

"Essentially don't do anything I wouldn't want someone doing to my sister if she was Elizabeth's age. Got it."

"It's good you understand." He strode to the door, opened it, and turned back inside. "Get down to the computer room. That's an order."

Roger nodded and hopped up. "You got it, Daniel."

13

———

"I'm surprised Danny doesn't mind your little smoking habit," Tanya said, her gaze glued to the monitor in front of her. Her hands flew across the keyboard as she spoke. "He hates booze. I'm not sure why he's giving you a pass on weed."

"I think I know why," Roger said. He looked to the left, blowing a cloud of smoke out of the window. His eyes relaxed and fell half closed. A smile appeared on his face. "He's in charge of mentoring me. I bet he probably doesn't want to be the one to tell the boss."

"Yeah?" Tanya asked. "Just be careful and get some spray stuff to cover that smell. If someone else finds out, you may not be so lucky." She took a deep breath. "How's the botnet fairing?"

"They detected our DDoSing their network, same as a few minutes ago. They shifted our attacks to a sinkhole, but I redirected it back."

"Just to be safe, switch periodically from SQLi and XSS. Don't give them a chance to acclimate," Tanya said.

They're amateurs over there," Roger said. "Our signal's

bounced across the globe. All they know is someone's slowing down their network. That's all. We're also aimed at the NSA and CIA. It's a hell of a smokescreen. Thank God for our budget."

"Good. I'm not seeing anything in the FBI database that would indicate they're interested in us." Her pinky smashed the space bar. "Wait a minute now. It says here they've sent an agent to question Alexander." She looked to Roger. "It's probably just a routine check. Right?"

"His political opponent's campaign manager just got jumped. Obviously he'd be the one they'd question first," Roger said. "I don't think that's a problem, considering he knew nothing about it. Still, we should probably report this and see what the higher ups think."

Tanya leaned back, arching her back against the computer chair. Her modest chest pushed against the thin fabric of her mauve shirt. She peeked over at Roger. "See something you like, or are you just too stoned and zoning out?"

Roger snapped back to the monitor, a blush appearing on his cheeks. "Maybe both," he said under his breath.

"At least you're honest, unlike that buffoon."

"You mean Daniel?" Roger asked.

"Sometimes I think he doesn't even know what he's feeling."

"I'll try and let him know you're interested then," Roger chuckled.

Tanya's arm reached out and slapped the back of Roger's head. "You'll do nothing of the sort, Mr. Giddy. Besides, who said I was interested in that dumbass?" She huffed and puffed her cheeks out.

"Who indeed?"

"Are you trying to be deep, or is that the drugs talking?"

"I don't know," Roger snickered. "Maybe both."

"And here I thought I'd never get to experience these thrilling philosophical discussions again after you got promoted. Don't quit your day job, Plato, and stop laughing so much." She turned, showing a beaming grin. "It's a dead giveaway." The two burst out laughing until a knock on the door quietened them.

"Sounds like you two are having fun in here," Daniel said, closing the door behind him. "Make any progress yet?"

Roger cleared his throat, extinguished the joint and tossed it out the window. "Yes, but we're not sure if it's good or bad."

"Explain," Daniel said.

"The FBI did in fact send an agent, but he's questioning our benefactor. He didn't know anything about your little visit to the Garrisan's did he?" Tanya asked, looking up from her station at Daniel.

Daniel rubbed his throat. "No, he had no idea. That's still not good, considering he's seen most of our faces. I'll tell dad and see what he thinks. Anything else happening?"

"Besides cyber attacking most of the alphabet agencies in a massive misdirection game for you guys?" Tanya asked, shifting her weight and letting her hands fall to her hips. "No, not really. We're just lucky the feds are transfixed on other issues, not their cyber security."

"What are they focused on anyway?" Roger asked.

Both turned to him and raised an eyebrow.

"Well, I'm just saying. You're looking at their files, right?"

"Oh, Lord," Daniel started. "Don't get her started on politics, please. You'll never shut her up."

Tanya stepped up to Daniel and stomped on his foot. "How rude."

Daniel hopped on one foot, cursing under his breath. "Jesus Christ! That hurt, you psycho bitch."

"I hope so," Tanya smirked. "Take a lesson from your buddy here and know when to shut up for once." She turned back to Roger. "To answer your question, it seems they're abandoning their initial modus operandi."

"Hmm?" Roger asked.

Tanya sat back down in her computer chair and spun to face the desktop. "Come and look."

Roger stood up and leaned down, looking over Tanya's shoulder at the monitor. "The FBI is not pursuing charges against Mr. Tracey since it was ruled gross negligence in handling classified material. What the hell? Isn't that shit illegal?"

"For us peons," Tanya said. "See, when the political elite -"

"I'm out of here." Daniel threw his arms above his head. "I've listened to this too many times. Have fun in conspiracy la-la land." Daniel stomped out of the room.

Tanya leaned up and gazed at Roger. "Want me to blow your mind? Do you know what the director of the FBI is caught up in right now?"

Bernard's office...

"This could be bad," Bernard grimaced. "If that yellow bellied, limp wristed shit talks, we're through." Bernard folded his hands in front of him. "I need to talk to him face to face. Tell the tech department to send an anonymous message." He scribbled a note in the open notebook on the desk. He tore off the page and shoved it across the table.

"Tell them to send this address with a request from me to meet. I cannot allow him to say anything. If he does, he goes six feet under. Understood?"

"I'll get on it right after I leave. Before I go, I have a question," Daniel said.

Bernard rubbed his forehead, wiping away the sweat forming. "What is it now? As if I don't have enough to worry about."

"Has Elizabeth talked to you recently?"

"No, why? What's going on with her now? Is someone giving her trouble?"

Daniel shook his head. "I took care of that, but she does seem to have a bit of a crush on the new guy."

"I don't care," Bernard said, massaging his temples. "I just don't care anymore. You make sure she doesn't get hurt. I have more important things to worry about. You understand me? You're her big brother. Act like it."

"I'll take care of it."

"Good." Bernard flung open the box at the corner of the desk and plucked a cigar out. He bit down on the end and rolled it around in his mouth. "Get a group of boys ready on the off chance the talks don't go as I expect. We'll have to dispose of any leaks in a timely manner. Get your prodigy in on it too. From what I see, he can take care of business."

"I'll get the best we have. Any plans in the meantime?"

"So long as you prepare, I don't care what you spend tonight doing. You're a big boy now. Act like it. Surprise me why don't you?"

"Need me to get your escort ready, Pop?" Daniel asked.

Bernard brushed a lock of gray hair back. "Don't underestimate your old man, boy. I may be getting older, but I can still assemble my own guard."

Daniel shrugged, a knowing smile plastered on his face. "Got to keep you on your toes, old man."

"Piss off," Bernard said with a smile.

———

Tech department...

"Do you see how he's actually covering up for him?" Tanya asked, bouncing in her seat.

"Why aren't people rioting? Is that not sedition?" Roger asked.

"People don't yell, scream, and fight anymore. All they say is, 'I feel safer already'. Too many people trust the government to have their best interests at heart, when they really -"

"Oh God damn, is she still at it?" Daniel asked, shoving the door open. "I told you not to get her started, bro. She never shuts up."

"I could say the same for you," Tanya grumbled. "What do you want now?"

Daniel snubbed his nose with his thumb. "We have another job on the horizon. For now, all we need is for you to send our benefactor this." He dug into his pants pocket and handed over the crumpled paper to Tanya's outstretched hand.

"What is that?" Roger asked.

"It looks like the big man wants to meet Mr. Alexander," Tanya said, typing into her keyboard and hitting enter. "Was this all?"

"No. In addition, we're getting ready in case he decides to talk."

Tanya pushed her chair back and jumped up. "We're

going to knock him off? I don't know about this plan. How's that going to look?"

"Bosses orders are law," Roger said, focusing on the open window. "You know how it goes."

"At least someone here has some sense," Daniel said. He stepped over the strewn wires and leaned down behind Tanya, looking at the monitor. "Good thing you haven't turned him into a raving lunatic yet with this crap."

"Just give her a little more time. She's working on it."

Tanya stuck her tongue out. "Why does everyone always gang up on me? I'm not crazy - I just spread the truth."

"Ask any person locked in a padded room, and they're likely to say the same." Daniel ruffled her hair.

She brushed his hand away. "Don't touch me."

"I think she's blushing, dude," Roger said.

"Just get out of here and plan your little potential assassination. You did come here to get your new partner, didn't you?"

"You sent the message, didn't you?" Daniel asked. He looked over as a beep from her computer interrupted him.

Tanya looked back at the screen. "He should be there according to the response I got. I made sure they knew it wasn't a choice." Tanya rubbed her elbow. "I feel a little dirty having to threaten his family though."

Daniel whistled. "Damn, girl. I don't remember saying to go full ruthless on them."

"It's always implied with you."

"I can't argue that." Daniel's eyes flicked to Roger. "Are you still needed here?"

"He wasn't ever 'needed', but yes, he's pretty much done."

"It's nice to feel loved," Roger quipped.

"Come on, lover boy. You're coming with me then."

Daniel reached down and hauled him out of the chair. "We're going to go have a little meeting."

"If I might make a suggestion, don't use a bullet for once," Tanya said, looking at the carpeted floor. "It'd look too obvious if you do decide to go through with it. Use a compound that would induce a heart attack, for example. Running a campaign is stressful after all."

"Noted," Daniel replied. He tugged Roger forward before twisting his neck back once they were half out the door. "What chemical would that be exactly?"

"Let me look it up and find the easiest to get. Shall I deliver it once I get it for you, master?" Sarcasm dripped from her voice.

"Yes, that'll work. In case that falls through, make sure we have some explosives too. Thanks," Daniel said before slamming the door shut.

"The one time he says thanks," she said to herself. She turned back to the monitor. "I guess I'm on research and procurement thanks to my big mouth and that dumbass."

14

"Can you believe what Bruce did to me?" Elizabeth asked looking away.

"What did he do now?" Roger asked the woman sitting beside him.

Elizabeth stole a glance, the side of her mouth angling up. Her lips quivered and a lone tear trailed down her cheek. "He..." she paused, "he tried to have his way with me."

Roger looked around the room's chattering occupants before looking back at the woman. "I don't know what to say. If you need me to -"

"Just keep him away from me." She looked up, looking him in the eye. "Please?"

He placed his hands on her shoulders. "Your brother set him straight, but if he gives you any more trouble, just tell me. I'll do what I can."

"You promise?" She asked, her voice mousey.

"Of course. I'll do everything in my power."

She leaned her head onto his chest. "Thanks."

A wolf whistle broke the tender scene, followed by a

male voice calling out. "Kiss her already, dingbat. She wants it." An uproarious roar of laughter followed.

Elizabeth dug her head out of Roger's chest. She turned to face them. The group fell silent and returned their attention back to the television.

"You have to teach me how to do that," Roger said.

"It doesn't take much to scare the rank and file." Her voice grew louder. "Sometimes I wonder if any of them are even really men." Her voice fell. "Not like you." She traced a finger down his chest.

"Every man has his faults. Some are just worse than others. You may be surprised by what you find."

Elizabeth stopped tracing his chest and rested her palm against it. "That sounds dangerous. It makes me curious about what you're hiding now."

"Maybe you'll find out someday. Just remember what I said."

She stood up and grabbed his hand. "Come with me. I want to show you something." She tugged his arm.

Roger stood up. "Of course. Lead the way." He followed behind, his hand still enveloped by her dainty appendage. "Where are we going?"

She led him up the main stairs and pushed open the double door. "Something every man here wants to see."

Bernard's door at the end of the hall opened. He strolled out and looked at the pair. His eyes fell on Roger as they passed in the hallway. He nodded and continued past.

Roger twisted his neck and looked at Bernard's retreating form. "What was that about I wonder?"

"I don't think I've ever seen daddy react that way when I was holding a guy's hand. He must like you. You know what that means?"

"I'll wake up tomorrow?"

Elizabeth yanked his hand forward, causing him to stumble. "That, and your prospects around here are looking good. Now come on already."

"Yes, ma'am."

Elizabeth's room...

"You weren't joking," Roger said. "Every man here would love to see this." He took in everything in the spacious room. "These ceilings must be 15 feet tall. Geez."

"Leave it to him to notice the damned ceiling first," Elizabeth said under her breath. She reached a hand into the chest of drawers. "I didn't bring you here to hear your opinions on interior design." She pulled out a flowing turquoise evening dress. She turned around and held the clothes up in front of her. "What do you think? Does it suit me?"

Roger's eyes traced her from head to toe. "You'd look wonderful in anything."

She stepped forward, swung a foot out, and nudged his leg. "That's not a real answer. Tell me what you really think."

"Alright, you asked for it." He brought a hand up and rubbed his chin. "Personally, I think you'd look dazzling in it. Though I'd prefer red and for it to be a little longer."

She burst out laughing.

"What? You said be honest."

She folded the clothing and placed it back inside the drawer. She shook her head and fell back on the bed beside him. "I guess that's what I get for asking a guy like you. Though I will say, you were more honest than anyone else I asked."

"How did they answer?"

She opened one eye and peeked at him. "They gave meaningless platitudes like you did at first. You were the first to suggest a different color would look better on me."

"This was a shit test, wasn't it?"

"A what?"

"You know how women will do something just to see how a guy reacts, then judge if they want to move forward.

"If it was..." Elizabeth trailed off, "then you passed."

"God knows how Bruce passed it. That dude has the tact of a bulldozer."

"He took a bit more of a direct approach. It caught me off guard."

Roger turned to her. "Interesting to know. Did it work?"

"You'd better be careful, mister. If you're thinking of trying the same thing, you should know that once you go there it's too late to back out." She rolled to face him. "So how about it?"

"I'll press my luck." He leaned forward until their lips met. He pulled back and saw her eyes closed. "Direct enough?" he asked in a whisper.

"Is that it? Pretty weak all in all," she purred.

He placed a hand on the back of her head. "Far be it from me to disappoint a lady." He gently guided her head forward until he seized her lips again, a husky moan escaping.

She climbed on top of him, sat up, and stared down at him. "Big words I've heard before. Let's see if you can live up to them." Her hand fell behind her. "Though from what I can feel, big guy, you might just be able to. Now let's see if that silver tongue knows how to move." She slid up...

Eddy's room...

"I don't know. She seems to like him." Daniel shrugged. "What do you think?"

"The latest word from the grapevine is that she dragged him to her room, brother. You want my honest opinion?" Eddy shifted his position with gritted teeth.

"Always."

"I'm a little worried for the kid, honestly. Your sis doesn't mess around. I wonder if he knows what he's getting involved in."

"He's a big boy. He knows what he's doing."

"You're probably right. Now moving on from that, mind if I ask you a question?"

"Shoot."

Eddy looked at the door and back at Daniel. "You were the one who beat the shit out of Bruce, weren't you?"

"Yeah. What of it?" Daniel crossed his arms.

"Why exactly? Did he get a little too fresh or something? You know the dude's always been like that since they got together."

"Lizzie told me what he did to her."

"Which was what, exactly?"

"That bastard forced her," Daniel looked down, "against her will."

"To hear her tell it," Eddy said.

"What exactly are you implying?"

Eddy scratched his nose. "I'm just saying that maybe you should look at everything before alienating one of your brothers in arms. It doesn't inspire loyalty if the boss doesn't have your back."

"If he did -"

"If he did, then he deserves that beating and more. Did you even ask before you laid into him?"

Daniel scratched the back of his neck and looked away.

"That's what I thought. If you want to lead, look at all the angles first. Your dad and I aren't trying to ball you out. We're trying to shape you into a leader. Now go talk to him and figure this shit out, because it can't keep going on this way."

"You always were a pain in the balls."

"Sometimes you need a good kick. You're too stubborn - the spitting image of your father."

"I'm going to pretend I didn't hear that."

Eddy reached out and clutched Daniel's arm. "One more thing. Your sister getting involved with your student? That's going to complicate everything for you. My advice? Either try and get them together for good or break them apart early - one or the other. This is no time for half measures. You understand?"

"Why?"

"Think about it. What happens if she gets tired of him and spreads another story? This time it gets to daddy, and then he looks at you. Why didn't you stop it?"

Daniel bit his lip. "Shit."

"Exactly. Just because this isn't a typical office romance doesn't make it any less complicated. That usually falls on the boss to mediate. Still looking forward to stepping up?"

Daniel snorted and turned to the door. "Don't worry about this. I'll take care of it right now. You just rest and get better." He stormed out of the room with a slam of the door.

"Sorry, kid, but this is for your own good," Eddy said to the empty room.

Just outside Elizabeth's room…

Daniel pounded on the mahogany door. "Open up, or I'm kicking it in." He tapped his foot and shifted his weight. He backed up a few steps. "Don't say I didn't warn you." He lurched forward with a mighty kick, flinging the door open and tumbling inside. He blinked, covered his eyes, and turned around. "Is there a reason you couldn't answer me, Sis? I get why he couldn't, but come on. I didn't have to see this. A simple 'one minute' would have sufficed." He retched and stumbled out of the door, slamming it behind him. Muffled whispering and shuffling could be heard inside.

The door squeaked open and a fully clothed Roger came outside, looking at the carpeting. He wiped his mouth. "I assume I know why you're here."

"Go brush your teeth and come back immediately. I need to speak to my sister first."

Roger took off into a jog down the hallway and disappeared behind the corner.

Daniel exhaled. "Shit." He knocked on the cracked open door. "Are you decent?"

"Thanks to you," Elizabeth's voice answered.

He pushed the door open and closed it behind him.

Elizabeth sat with her legs crossed, clad only in a bathrobe. "What the fuck was so important that you had to interrupt us in the middle?"

"You're serious about him?"

"What business is that of yours?" she huffed.

Daniel leaned against the door. "Simple. It could blow back on me later."

"You're worried I'm going to embarrass you through your little protégé? Did it ever occur to you that maybe I actually like him?"

"Just don't do what you did with Bruce. Alright?"

"What is that supposed to mean?"

"Nothing."

Elizabeth stood up and moved in front of Daniel. "Who I get involved with is no concern of yours or daddy's. You get me?"

"All I ask is that if you do break up with him down the line, do it on the down low."

"Of course that's what you're worried about. Would it surprise you if I said I was maybe a little serious with him?"

"You're serious?"

"Well, why not? He's a nice enough guy, unlike most of you savages."

Daniel smirked. "How much do you even know about him anyway? I bet you wouldn't be so head over heels if you knew what his hobbies are."

She blew a lock of dark hair out of her face. "It couldn't be worse than the other guys here."

"In that case it's good. I want to see you happy after all. Just don't say I didn't warn you. You might not like what you find."

"Are you going to give him the same speech after this?"

Daniel kicked off the wall and walked to the door. "I'm an equal opportunities kind of guy, so sure."

Elizabeth hopped off the bed. "Danny, don't touch him. I mean it."

"My baby sis's wishes shall be heeded. Don't worry. He's my friend too. I just want to be sure nobody gets hurt down the line."

"Bullshit. You're looking out for number one down the line."

"Tomato, tomahto." He exited without further ado and

saw Roger jogging down the corridor toward him. "Come here a minute."

Roger stopped in front of him.

Daniel turned him around and walked down the hallway side by side, a hand planted on Roger's shoulder. "Do you remember what I said to you before? Because I don't remember saying 'I like you. You can come home and fuck my sister'."

"Don't screw around with her?"

"So what do you call what you were doing?"

Roger gulped. "Going with the flow?"

Daniel brought his free hand and covered his eyes. "I never heard it called that before." He squeezed Roger's shoulder causing a flinch. "It's so nice to have a future brother-in-law in the wings."

"Brother-in-law?" Roger asked, his hands beginning to shake.

"You are serious with her." He squeezed even tighter, his teeth gritting, "Right, brother?"

Roger glanced out the window to his right and back to Daniel. "Of course."

Daniel slapped Roger's back. "Good. Now that that's settled, I guess I'll let you get back to your dinner. I'll come knocking when I have a job for you two. Just answer next time. Got it? There are some things a man ought not see. Like his sister nude. I blame you for that by the way."

"Me? Why me?"

Daniel didn't answer except for a narrow-eyed glare.

"O-okay."

15

"He just barged in? Good Lord." Tanya fanned her face with her hand. "Does that doofus not know common manners?"

Elizabeth crossed one leg over the other. "Well, he did knock."

"Why didn't you answer?"

"I was," Elizabeth's cheeks flushed a brilliant crimson, "busy and didn't hear him."

"He just busted in mid org-" she covered her mouth. "At least Rog apparently knows more about how to please a woman than I thought."

"What was that?" Elizabeth's eyes narrowed. "You two were together?"

"Oh my, no. We used to joke about how perfect we'd be together is all." She looked away and forced another laugh.

Elizabeth tilted her nose up. "Good. Don't get any ideas. He's mine now. Don't you or any other girl here forget it."

Tanya swiveled her chair in a circle. "So long as you two are happy, I'm cool. I know everything about the goof. Just ask me if you need something."

A chime interrupted Tanya. She spun to face the monitor and leaned forward. "I just got an update from the field. Apparently the talk with our ex KGB contacts went well."

"Those meatheads?" Elizabeth asked, leaning back in the computer chair. "They can run guns and lift weights with the best of them, but when it comes to conversation they're as dull as paint."

"It's a good thing he negotiated a contract for said guns then. Loads of them of the automatic rifle variety according to this. We've set up the foundation. Now if Alexander wins and follows through, we're set to make a killing with this racket. That is, if you can trust a slimy weasel like him to actually get it done."

"He'll get it done. If not, his family may have a tragic accident." Elizabeth pulled her vibrating phone out of her pocket, pushed a button, and stared at the screen. She rolled her eyes.

Tanya blew a pink bubble and popped it. "Something happening?"

"Just need to clean up after my bonehead brother. I'm off to pick up Rog and head out."

Tanya cracked her knuckles. "Guess that means I should get back to work too. Just make sure not to wear him out too much. I'd hate for you two to be late for whatever that blithering fool wants."

"That'd be a real shame."

Inside Elizabeth's sports car...

"Just wondering since I never heard you say, why did you join?" Elizabeth asked, flicking the turn signal. A constant clicking echoed around the car.

"Remember how I told you I have a sister?" Roger asked.

Elizabeth reached a hand up and readjusted the mirror. "Yeah. What about her?"

"She has cystic fibrosis. Mix that with my parents both being out of a job, and you can begin to see why," Roger said, his tone docile as he stared at the cityscape rushing by to his right. He leaned against his elbow as he spoke. "Me and Tanya did a bit of research, and, come to find out, the first round of a new experimental drug costs over one hundred thousand dollars."

"I can't tell if you're selfless or just plain idiotic."

Roger snapped to attention and glared at her. "Excuse me? What did you say?"

"You gave up a normal life for your sister; and, to top it off, they kicked you out. Seems like a pretty shitty deal. What are you going to do? Force them to take your blood money? If they're as 'moral' as you make them out to be, there's no way they'll take it." She glanced over and tilted her head. "Just being honest."

"You're not wrong. I'll figure out a way. Cryptocurrency has come a long way at least."

"So, let's say you get the dough. What then? You know you're never going back to that life."

Roger stared forward, not focusing on anything. "I hadn't thought that far ahead to be honest."

"At least you're trying, I guess. That means something to me at least. I'm sure your sister will see it the same way eventually."

Roger reclined the chair. "Eventually?"

"She just lost her brother because her mom and dad

kicked him out. She's going to be pissed off, boy let me tell you. When she learns why, she'll probably hate you too for forcing them to."

"Fantastic. At least she'll be alive to hate me."

Elizabeth stepped on the brakes, bringing the vehicle to a stop. "You're the weirdest guy I've ever met."

"I think I'll take that as a compliment." He opened the door and stepped out. He looked over the orange, low-sitting car and saw Elizabeth surveying the neighborhood. "Any idea what we're doing here?"

"Danny said to get here pronto. He should have been here to meet us." She pointed to a tall, abandoned building. "I think he's in there."

"An abandoned building?" Roger asked. He removed one of his revolvers and moved beside Elizabeth. "Just stay close. I have a bad feeling about this."

Elizabeth clasped her hands. "My knight in shining armor." She shoved him aside. "Ease off, big boy."

"Why me?" Roger asked himself and trotted off to catch up. He caught up as she approached the door. "At least let me go in first."

She gestured ahead. "Go ahead, big man."

He inched the glass door open and skulked inside the pitch-black interior. "Daniel?" he called out. "You there, buddy?"

He felt a soft, warm embrace wrap around him from behind. His back straightened. "What the hell?" He wriggled in the grip but was held firmly in place. A warm breathy whisper crawled into his ears. "I said to take it easy, didn't I? You're going to give yourself a heart attack." He was released and stumbled forward until he regained his balance.

"I don't like this setup," Roger mumbled. "It doesn't make any sense."

"Danny always did have a flair for the dramatic. He's probably further inside." She hitched onto his left arm and snuggled close. "Let's go."

Roger saw a small white screen to his left illuminate the area around them. He reached and covered the screen. "Don't."

"I can't see. Why not?" she asked.

"It lights us up. In the off chance this is a setup, it's basically saying 'shoot here'."

Elizabeth shook her head and shoved the phone back inside her pants. "You're paranoid, but alright, sure. You can be the boss here, my dutiful bodyguard."

Roger kept his revolver at the ready as he led them forward. He was stopped as the metal pushed against something solid. He wrenched his other hand free and groped around until he found a metallic feeling object waist high. He turned it and pushed forward, eliciting a piercing creak. He heard a click and, without warning, shoved Elizabeth down. He landed on top of her as a thunderous boom erupted. The door flung forward and bounced onto Roger.

A low voice could be heard. "If you're hearing this, you're probably in shock and dying. Did you Morris types really think we were just going to take your assault on Enforcer territory unchallenged? Don't worry. I'll let daddy dearest know his little girl won't be coming home. Count on it, darling." The recording ended, leaving only the sounds of grunts.

"You alright?" Roger's strained voice whispered.

"Yeah. Now get off me."

"One thing at a time." Roger fell to the side, causing the

door to clatter to the ground. He flopped onto the cold concrete of the warehouse ground, unmoving.

Elizabeth rolled to the side, sat up, and dusted herself off. "That fucker's dead for this." She looked over through the smoky interior filled with dust particles. "Rog?" When no reply came, she crawled over and placed a hand on his neck. "Still breathing at least." She shoved the door the rest of the way off him. "Don't worry." She rested a hand on his shoulder. "I'll get you out of here somehow." She looped an arm over her shoulders and grunted in exertion as she tried to raise him. She dropped back to the ground. "You're too heavy. Dragging it is then." She reached her arms under his and dragged him back the way they had come. She backed out of the building and propped him up against the side of her sports car. She flung open the passenger door and managed to eventually get him inside. "Wait until Danny hears about this shit." She got into the driver's seat and sped off.

At the compound...

"What are you talking about? You're hysterical," Daniel said as he was being dragged by Elizabeth out to her car. "Oh my God," he said, stepping outside and seeing Roger's drooping figure in the front seat. "Is he alive?"

"He took the brunt of the blast. He needs a doc now."

Daniel flung the door open. "I'm not even going to ask where you were or why you dragged him there, but Dad will. Count on that. Now help me get him inside."

The two dragged him inside. Daniel screamed as they

entered the foyer. "Get over here and get him upstairs to the doc. That was not a request, boys."

The men nearby who were channel surfing hopped up and swarmed the group. They soon snatched him from their hands and were dragging him away. The door slammed, leaving just the twins standing in the monstrous living room.

Daniel placed his hands on his hips. "You want to tell me what happened? Why were you two even out?"

"I got a text from someone I thought was you telling us to head there."

"Considering it wasn't my phone number, I question why you'd believe that."

Tanya's bubbly voice spoke out after a prolonged creak. "Someone has never heard of spoofing numbers." She skipped down the stairs and stopped a few feet away. "They didn't just fool her, they got me at first glance too. Essentially, it looked like it was indeed your number."

"Fine," Daniel said. "So, what happened to your boyfriend once you got there?"

Elizabeth pursed her lips. "He tried to play the tough guy hero type. You know, 'Get behind me' and such. He led the way inside. We groped around in the dark and found another door. He opened it and jumped on top of me after that damned click."

"Rawr." Tanya meowed with a swat of her hand. She looked at the twins who were glaring at her. "Sorry. Serious time it is."

"Anyway, after the click an admittedly weak explosion rocked the area. A recording came on directly after. It was the Enforcer's getting back at us for before. They tried to assassinate me to retaliate against Daddy."

"Those fucking animals." Daniel's hands balled into fists.

"You don't go after a man's family and expect to get away with it. Maybe it's time to teach them the same lesson."

"I'm going with you," Elizabeth said. She walked toward the stairs, only to have Daniel place a hand on her shoulder as she passed, stopping her. "Don't even try it. They want me, they're going to regret that wish."

"Settle down. I'll bring it up to Dad. You just go and sit beside your boyfriend's sick bed. He'll love that."

"I'm not sure whether I should call that sexist or thoughtful," Tanya said.

"How about we both tell Dad, and maybe I'll do that?" Elizabeth asked, shoving past Daniel.

"She's always so stubborn," Daniel said before taking off into a jog up the stairs behind his sister.

"She's not the only one," Tanya remarked under her breath.

Daniel caught up with her at the top of the stairs and followed her through the doors. "Just let me do the talking, alright?"

"So you don't get blamed I assume?" Elizabeth asked. "He needs to know everything that happened." They approached the familiar double doors.

The man standing outside stretched out a palm. "Wait a moment. The boss is in the middle of very important phone calls at the moment and he -"

"Not the time, jackass." Elizabeth pushed him aside and threw the door open.

Bernard kicked his legs up onto the desk as he spoke into the phone at his ear. "It's always a pleasure, Ivan. Yes. Make sure you send my warmest regards for that delicious meal from your dear mother. It was scrumptious and really helped our negotiations. Uh huh. I'll talk to you later. Something's come up over here." He pressed a button and placed the phone down. "What is it? It'd better be important."

Daniel stomped up to the desk and slammed his palms down. "We may want to hold off breaking out the champagne bottles."

"What happened now?"

"Liz here," Daniel jabbed a finger over his shoulder, "was just lured to an abandoned warehouse and got a real blast for a welcome. Thank God Rog was there, or who knows what would have happened."

Bernard's eyes grew wide and he bared his teeth. "What the fuck were you doing going out anyway?"

Elizabeth peeked over her brother's shoulder. "Daddy, I -"

"As I was saying, they lured her there, Pops. They spoofed my number. She thought I was calling for backup."

"Underhanded little slugs." Bernard looked up at his daughter. "And you're alright?"

Elizabeth nodded but kept her gaze on the desk.

"This couldn't happen at a worse time. If we respond, everything gets put in jeopardy."

"It'll never be traced back to Alexander, Dad. What's the problem?" Daniel asked.

"The city is voting at the end of the week, and he asks me what's the problem. Think about it, moron. If we show our asses and fire back, it escalates into an all-out war. If we do nothing, they piss on us and go after you again. Our benefactor, Mr. Alexander, does not want us in the news for obvious reasons. You starting to see the problem?" He exhaled and leaned back in the lavish seat. "Damned if I do, damned if I don't."

"Dad," Daniel started, "let me just take a group of boys

and cut the head off their organization. That way it'll be over before it even starts."

"We don't even know where their shot callers are, Son. You'd be groping blindly and would probably start a shit storm that we can't afford right now. They know that too, the sons of bitches." Bernard pounded a fist into his palm. "If I could get my hands on that bombing asshole…"

"We can't just let this go." Daniel leaned forward. "What will people think?"

"You leave that to me. That's my job. Your job is to do what I say. Don't forget that. Now get out. I have more phone calls to make, thanks to this. I'll fix it, somehow. Just don't start any more shit. That's an order."

Recovery room…

"They used a blooming bomb to go after Lizzie?" Eddy asked. "Hell, Danny must have flipped his lid, not to mention the boss. No wonder she was sleeping on your chest earlier. She's grown attached to you. It was really a moving scene, if I do say so. She just snuggled up on your chest as you both slept. It brought a smile to this old man's face." Eddy wiped a nonexistent tear away.

"I've no memory of any of that. The last thing I remember was a clicking sound, and I woke up here talking to you." He blinked and, rubbing his eyes, surveyed the room. "I don't see Elizabeth anywhere. Hopefully that means she's resting somewhere more comfortable."

Eddy looked to his right at the other bedridden occupant. "Kid, you've been the talk of the place all day. The boys are calling you her bodyguard extraordinaire. You're just lucky you're not dead, jumping on top of her like that and taking the brunt of the blast wave."

Roger scratched his stubble. "Oh boy. I did that?"

"Yep, saved her in the process. I hope you're ready for what that means. You poor, virtuous bastard. You're going to learn kindness isn't always best here."

"Do what now?"

"See, she gets attached easily. Her last target was Bruce. You remember that fiasco? Well, he never did much for her. I shudder to think how she's going to treat you now. I sincerely hope you like her, because you're stuck with her now. On the bright side, the boss loves you I'd imagine."

"I just acted on instinct. Nothing special."

"You just make sure to write your family after this and tell them you're alright. They're probably worried sick, especially that adorable little sister. She'd be bawling her little eyes out if she were here right now I bet."

Roger blew a hair out of his eyes. "You're probably right about Michelle. I should let her know I'm alright. I just hope she's alright without me being there. She never remembers to put that damned mask on before bed. Dad always forgets. If nothing else, I can use it as an excuse to remind her."

"She needs a mask?" Eddy asked, his eyebrow rising.

"An oxygen mask, yes. Otherwise, she'd possibly suffocate in the middle of the night."

"Shit, man. That's rough. They kicked you out?"

Roger looked over and glared.

"It's common knowledge around here now. That's another lesson. Nothing is ever private here. Word always gets around."

"Yeah, apparently organized crime wasn't part of their plan for their baby boy. They disowned me when they found out I'd been taken in by you boys. To be honest, I don't really blame them. They made a good point. I'd have been a threat to Michelle just by being around her."

"I hear that. It's funny how many of us have been kicked out from our biological families. That's why we always look out for each other. We're all we've got left for many of us."

"What about you? If you don't mind my asking, what's your story?" Roger asked.

Eddy snorted and looked down at his lap. "Me? I guess fair's fair. I fell in with the Morris family at a young age. My family is a lot like most. We always needed more money - sis needed ballet shoes, the dog needed a vet visit. You know the drill. My dad was a notorious drunk and couldn't hold down a job, so I decided to take matters into my own hands. The only problem was, no one wanted to hire a fourteen-year-old. So I headed down to the local Morris hangout and let it be clear I wanted to work. They had me running numbers and delivering coded messages for years until I worked my way up to parking cars and beyond. From there my story mirrors yours, minus the sick sister. They kicked me out when they found out how I was earning their living."

"They stuck me in front of a computer screen when I joined up at eighteen. How did the physical errands pay, out of curiosity?"

Eddy chortled. "A couple of g's a month."

"Flipping hell, you got the sweet gig then. They only paid me a thousand a month."

"You only sat in front of a computer next to that hottie downstairs though. I was dodging the 5-0 daily. You were dodging what? Antiviruses?"

Roger sat up, a wide grin appearing. "Motherfucker, have you ever learned how to direct a botnet under the tutelage of that crazy girl? Much gnashing of teeth and screeches were had, let me tell you. And that was only during the script kiddie portion of my education."

They both burst into laughs.

"At least you're getting out of here tonight," Eddy said. "With this cast, I'm stuck in here for another day before I can even begin to take a piss on my own."

"You'll be up and dodging more gunfire sooner than you think. Enjoy the opportunity to take it easy, bro."

"That goes double for you. You're in the big time now. Each week's paycheck may be five to ten thousand, but that won't mean much if you get pinched or wasted. I'm sure your sister would rather have her big brother than medicine. Never forget what's important. Family trumps all else."

16

"Are you sure you're alright for duty? It's only been a day," Daniel asked.

Roger rubbed his head. "Doc said it was a minor concussion from the blast. So long as I don't get another whack to the head, I should be fine."

Daniel scoffed. "That won't happen." He wiped his nose. "By the way, I've been wanting to say something to you." The pair stopped in the middle of the remote hallway. "Don't tell anyone I said this, but thanks for watching out for Liz before." He looked away. "If you weren't there, she'd probably be dead. That means something to me."

"Anytime, brother," Roger said with a step forward as they kept walking. "So, what's the next job?"

"Dad called the Enforcers a little while ago. We should have our marching orders soon enough. Though to be frank, I doubt it's going to be a kill order. We apparently need to tone down the noise with the election coming up, even though they tried to kill my baby sister. That needs to be made right. Don't you agree?"

"I'm biased, but yes. I think that was an asshole move that needs answered."

Daniel stopped near a large window at the end of the hall and peered out over the emerald fields of grass and treetops. He knocked on the glass with one hand and spoke. "That's right. They went after you and your girl. A real man has to let them know that's not acceptable. Any man here would understand that, even my father." He glanced to his side at Roger. "Are you thinking what I'm thinking?"

"As much as I'd love to end them, won't that get us, meaning me, in deep shit?" Roger asked. "If the boss is saying no, who am I to do it anyway?"

"You have a lot to learn about the politics around here, my friend. It's true, Dad is the final authority around here. He also has a soft spot for those who are loyal. You saved Eddy, Dad, and Elizabeth. Combine that with my backing, and nothing will happen to you. I personally guarantee it." He slapped Roger's shoulder, a toothy smile beaming all the while. "What do you say?"

Roger looked at Daniel and then back out the window. The corner of his mouth tilted up and he turned to Daniel. "Someone's got to keep you out of trouble. Who are we bringing?"

Daniel laughed out loud. "That's my man. Here's the plan..."

An Hour Later...

"We're going where?" Bruce asked, crossing his arms. "Besides, is this even sanctioned? Rumor was we were leaving well enough alone."

Daniel stood in front of the podium at the front of the room, Roger on his right. "You're just fine with them bombing Lizzie and getting away scot-free then?"

Bruce fell silent. His eyes fell to his shoes.

"That's right. Now the hard part will be finding the sons of bitches responsible. We have no real clue where their shot callers are. Thankfully, we do have the best and the brightest working on it."

Tanya blew a bubble and popped it. She looked up from her laptop. "What the hell am I doing?" she asked herself. "They did go after Liz, so they deserve it. Right?"

"You're standing up for your best friend so that she doesn't keep being targeted," Daniel said. "Don't forget that."

Bruce raised his hand. "I don't like your sister being bombed either, but I have a question. You and your little protégé may get out of this unscathed, but what about the rest of us?" He gestured to himself and Tanya sitting beside him. "We're just supposed to piss off the boss for you?"

"You don't know my father," Daniel said. "Do you really think he'll be mad at the men and women who took down the people who tried to assassinate his little girl? He'll be peeved at first, but he'll be fine with it."

"You hope. An easy position to take when he's your dad," Bruce said.

"Enough." Daniel slammed his fist into the podium. "Are you in or not?"

Bruce grumbled under his breath before nodding.

"Good. Now this will be simple. Once we get their location, we go and we wipe them out. We'll be taking the van for this one since we'll need the storage space. We've already got the shovels, duct tape, and extra magazines tucked away in the back."

"How are we cleaning up afterward?" Bruce asked. "Surely we're not going to bury a dozen people?"

"Why not?" Daniel asked through his teeth. "They tried to kill my sister and Rog here. Besides, I outrank you. Deal with it. You're going with us, and that's that. I'll take responsibility." He stepped around the podium and towered over Bruce. He leaned over and stared him down. "Is that enough for the coward?"

"It's fine," Bruce blurted out.

Daniel returned to his original position. "I'm glad we have your approval finally. You're going to oversee the van. Easy enough, right? Don't leave us, and try not to get shot. Simple enough for you? We may ask you to sack up and shoot at some point. Can you handle that?"

"I've got it already," Bruce huffed.

"If I'm allowed to finish..." Daniel cleared his throat. "After we get there, me, Rog, and yes even you, Bruce, are going to take them out before they even know what's happening. No firefights this time if all goes according to plan. Still, I recommend picking up a vest downstairs before we go, just to be safe."

"Not to interrupt this speech, but I have news." Tanya placed the laptop down on the seat beside her and jumped up. "I found where their online persona was logging in from, but that's as good as I could get. According to my ip trace and our past reports, it's near their territory, so I believe it's legitimate. There's just one problem."

"You can't be sure it wasn't just a troll who happens to live nearby," Roger spoke up. "Right?"

"Yeah, who'd imagine a person being bored enough to impersonate a criminal organization online?" Bruce asked.

"It happens more often than you might think," Roger said. "Some people want attention at any cost, and that's a great way to get it. Bonus points if their ip address matches with the group's territory."

"Bingo." Tanya snapped her fingers. "The location does give me some confidence. It's traced back to a dingy hole in the wall. Perfect for the Enforcers if I had to guess, but it is only a guess."

"Now we have our location, gentlemen. There's only one way to find out. Let's go already."

---

30 minutes later in the van...

"This looks like the place." Bruce stepped on the brakes and parked on the side of the road. "It looks ghetto enough for me to believe they hang here." His neck craned as he looked at the run-down bar with a flickering neon light in the window.

"Appearances can be deceptive," Roger said, rubbing the back of his head. "Believe me, I learned that last night. These cowards will do anything to end you or me."

"Ain't that the truth," Daniel said from the front. "We're just returning the favor. Now remember, we're outnumbered. We're not aiming for a firefight here, boys. It's a simple in and out. Bruce, go and see if this is even the right place."

Bruce twisted the key, yanked it free, and laid it in the cup holder. "Why me? This is your idea."

Daniel reached over and clutched Bruce's collar, pulling him across the gap in the seats. He gritted his teeth and a growl escaped his mouth. "Do it because I said so."

"Alright already." He pulled himself free and straightened out his jacket.

"Remember, he looks like this." Roger shoved his phone up front and showed the geriatric, wrinkled face on the screen.

"That's el Jefe," Daniel said, reclining in his seat. "Make a note where he is and come straight back here. I don't care if you peek in the windows or get a god-damned drink and come back. Just make sure the intel is good."

"I'll be right back then." Bruce threw the door open and crossed the road. He opened the stained-glass door and disappeared inside.

"Think he'll be alright?" Roger asked, kicking his feet up between the seats. He pulled out his red mask and slid it over his head as they waited.

"He bitches a lot, but he's a tough bastard," Daniel said, putting on his own black mask. "Besides, he deserves it after the way he treated my sister. You heard the rumor he was cheating on her?"

"He was? With who?" Roger asked.

"I don't know, but he got off easier than the last guy who was unfaithful to her. He knows that. That's why he kowtowed so quickly to what I said. He's lucky to still be breathing. Let that be a lesson. You're a part of my family now, for all intents and purposes. Don't fuck that up." He looked up at the rear-view mirror.

"I'd never hurt her."

"I know. That's why I sent him. He's disposable to me - you're not." He turned around in his seat. "You stick with me, and we'll rule this city. We'll get your sister all the meds she needs and look damn good doing it."

The driver's door opened, and Bruce plopped into the seat. "Found him. He's sitting with his back to that wall, about halfway deep in the room." He pointed to the left side of the building. "There's a window directly behind him and one across the room. So, what's the plan?"

"You're sure it was him?" Daniel asked, leaning forward toward Bruce.

"Positive. The old fart is recognizable with his gang of muscled bruisers sitting around him all sporting their colors. They're not subtle."

"Okay," Daniel said. "Here's the plan. Me and Rog are going over to the window directly behind him. We're going to blow his head off, run back, and you're going to get us out of here. Simple, right?"

"I knew I should have gotten a drink while I was in there," Bruce sighed. "Yeah, I got it. Just make sure you don't miss. They looked strapped with automatic pistols. You'll be swiss cheese if they get to retaliate. Make it quick. I'll leave the engine running."

"Then we're off. Let's go, Rog." Daniel swung the door open along with Roger in the back. They both slammed the doors shut and crossed the desolate, cracked street. "Look at these animals." Daniel kicked a stray plastic bag floating down the sidewalk. "They don't even try and clean up. You'd think they'd have some pride."

"Men who use bombs rarely cite pride when asked why," Roger said. "Besides, if they really cared, they'd replace that flashing neon sign. That reeks of poverty. They don't care. They must think it's a great camouflage."

"As usual, their low IQ betrays them," Daniel smirked. He reached over and jabbed Roger in the chest. "It just brings attention. Am I right?"

The pair entered the dim alley beside the broken-down building. They peeked in as they passed each window on their right.

"Hold up." Daniel extended an arm and stopped Roger.

He positioned himself beside the window, with Roger on the other side. "I think we found him." He peeked in the window. 'Yeah, that's his posse alright." He reached down into his belt, retrieved his pistol, and cocked it.

"Whoa, easy," Roger said, peeking himself. "I have an idea, but I'm not sure it's a good one."

"Spit it out."

"He loves using bombs, right? What say we utilize those stoves back there?"

"You mean cut the gas line or something?" Daniel asked.

"Turnabout's fair play. Am I right? Besides, I don't see any civilians in there. It'll just look like a gas leak. If we play it right, the boss won't even know we were here," Roger said.

"How would that even work?"

"Look, it's easy. We go in the back over there," Roger pointed past Daniel further in the alley, "and convince the chef or whoever the hell to get out. I cut the cord. Then the next time someone lights up a smoke in there it goes up. Simple. I mean, there's even a guy smoking as we speak. We can do this. Trust me."

Daniel lowered his weapon. "The path of least resistance is always best. We'll do it your way. Let's go." He led the pair behind the building, keeping low as they went. They turned the corner, and Daniel stood in front of the lone door.

Said door opened, and a short man carrying a large box appeared and descended the stairs. "I fucking hate garbage duty," he muttered to himself.

"Well then, good news." Daniel grabbed his arm and yanked, causing the box to tumble to the ground. "You get an early night off tonight, courtesy of us. Aren't we nice?"

The man's eyes danced between the two men. "Who are you, and what are you talking about?"

Daniel raised his 9mm and leveled it at the man.

His knees shook and he gulped audibly. "Okay, man. Just don't shoot me. I'll go."

Roger stepped forward, placed his hand on the man's back, and pushed him back where they came from. "Get out then, and don't worry about coming back tomorrow."

"You're too nice," Daniel scoffed.

"Yeah, that's why I recommended we blow up the building with everyone in it," Roger said, sarcasm dripping from his voice.

"Enough messing around. Let's get this started." Daniel climbed the stairs, Roger on his tail.

***

Back in the van a while later...

"They went around the side a while ago," Bruce said into the phone. "They should have been done by now."

"Did you hear their gunfire?" Tanya asked over the phone.

"I ain't heard shit." Bruce clicked his tongue. "I saw some guy run out of the alley, but that's it. What the hell are they doing back there?"

"Changing the plan it sounds like," Tanya said, her voice dour. "If they're not lighting them up, then I'd imagine Rog had a bright idea. Wait a minute..." she trailed off. The sound of clacking keys filled the speaker. "He wouldn't be dumb enough to try that. Would he?"

"Try what, exactly?" Bruce asked.

"It's a bar, slowpoke. It probably has a grill or something for food. The gas line could cause an explosion, keeping suspicion from falling on us, and explaining the bodies inside. Think about it." She paused and caught her breath. "Can you see them from where you are?" Tanya asked.

Bruce turned and looked out the foggy window. "They were standing near the back and just disappeared, presumably in the back door. Why? I'm not going in there again. Not after Mr. Morris ordered me to be on driving duty."

"Were there any innocents in there?"

Bruce flicked the heating on. "No, just a group of guys who gave me the stink eye. I got out of there as soon as I could."

"Okay, fine. I wish I'd known ahead of time, but fine. We can work with this."

"I'm just driving, lady. I don't care what happens so long as it works and I go home tonight." Bruce leaned his head back on the seat and looked back at the building. A man stood at the window staring out at him. "I'm getting a weird vibe here."

"What's happening?" Tanya asked between keys tapping in the background.

"One of the jacked thugs inside is eyeing me up and down. He's just standing there, watching me from inside the window."

"He's probably just waiting and watching for you to leave. If you were the only new guy, it makes sense. Just don't look him in the eye or something."

"Why's that?" Bruce asked.

"In the animal kingdom, eye contact is interpreted as aggression." Tanya's bubbly giggle reached his ear. "I think the same rule applies to the concrete jungle. You'd be the authority on that, not me. I'm just a little ole' tech girl."

"You're a smart ass is what you are."

"Better than being a dum-" The pair was interrupted by

the backdoors shooting open. Roger jumped in alongside Daniel.

"Go, go, go, asshole!" Roger kicked the driver's seat and slammed the door shut."

Bruce stepped on the gas. "What's the big idea?"

A massive explosion erupted behind them along with the sound of glass shattering.

"Well shit," Bruce said below his breath.

_____

17

"There's no one else back here," Roger said, surveying the cramped room. He walked between rows of appliances before stopping and bending over the back of the oven. "Ah, here we go." He extended his hand out. "You got a knife?"

"Here." Daniel unsheathed his serrated blade and handed it over, handle first. "Before you do that though, shouldn't you like plan ahead?"

Roger paused. "I never did this before." He stood up straight. "I suppose so." His hand fell into his pocket. "Here we go. I've got it." He fished out his metal lighter. "We're going to need a spark to light this baby up without us being here." He looked across the room at the only other door. He pointed and hurried over. "Look here. We can rig this door to my lighter so that when someone enters, they flick the wheel. We just need to find something to tie it with."

Daniel pivoted around scanning the room before marching to one side, grabbing an apron off a set of hooks, and heading back. He held his hand out. "Will this do?"

"Yeah, now just give me a sec." Roger tied the thin string

to the wheel, tied the other end to the doorknob, and set the lighter down on the nearby counter. "There. Now to just cut the line and get out." He ran over to the oven and leaned down behind it. "Be ready to run."

Daniel backed up a step. "Trust me. You don't have to tell me twice."

"There." Roger tossed the knife back to Daniel and took off into a sprint toward the door. "Now go."

The two barreled out of the door and slammed it behind them. As they passed the windows they saw the door opening. Roger placed a hand on Daniel's shoulder and fell. "Get down. The door's opening." The two flopped onto the concrete and laid there for a full minute in the freezing night air.

"Well? Where's the boom?" Daniel asked. He pushed Roger off him and dusted himself off.

Roger got to his feet and peeked into the window. "I don't think the lighter sparked. I can't see it anymore. Time for plan B." He reached into his coat and pulled out his revolver.

"Whoa, now," Daniel said. "A bullet won't ignite gas, will it?"

"No, but I need to get the window open and toss in a match. I don't fancy tearing my arm up." He reached into his other pocket and handed Daniel a pack of matches. "Take one, strike it, and prepare to throw it in on my signal. Then we hightail it out of here. Agreed?"

Daniel extracted a red tipped stick from the package and ignited it by striking the back of the case. "Ready."

Roger slammed the glass with the butt of his gun and shattered it. He got clear and prepared to run.

Daniel tossed in the fire and they both took off toward the van...

In the van, heading back to the compound...

"Did you really think tying an apron to your lighter would work?" Bruce erupted into laughter. "Oh man, that's great. It fell on the floor, didn't it? I bet it fell on the floor and the guy was like 'What the hell?'" He burst into another round of snickers. "Still, you can't argue with those results."

"I just hope the boss doesn't mind it too much," Roger said. He tapped his fingers on his knee. "It won't blow back on us, so he shouldn't. Then again, you two know him better than I do."

"Just leave that to me. I'll handle him," Daniel said. "I'm taking responsibility for it. It was my idea after all."

"Let's just hope your sister forgives you for dragging him along," Bruce snorted. "She's not the type who likes her man out at all hours of the night, kid. Trust me."

"Stop trying to scare him." Daniel looked over and elbowed Roger in the side. "He's not lying, but that's your battlefield, not mine."

"Not even a little advice?" Roger asked.

"Beg forgiveness," Bruce and Daniel answered in unison.

"I didn't do anything wrong. I just followed your orders to the T," Roger whined.

Bruce shook his head and smiled. "The kid's got a lot to learn about the family, doesn't he?"

"Yeah," Daniel said. "That's why he's got us." He gave a playful punch to Roger's shoulder. "Ain't that right, Rog?"

"I don't know what I'd do without you," Roger said. His sarcastic tone was accentuated by a roll of his eyes. "Shut up already."

The group fell into laughter and drove off into the darkness.

Bernard's office

"So, you three decided to blow the building up?" Bernard leaned forward and planted his elbows on the desk. "Under whose orders, exactly? I ask because I damned sure don't remember authorizing this. I didn't, did I?"

Daniel stood with Roger and Bruce on either side. "Mine. It was my idea for what they did to Lizzie."

"I see." Bernard stood up and paced back and forth. "You took it upon yourself to do my job for me. Is that it?"

"Dad, it's going to look like a gas explosion. Besides, they tried to kill your girl. We couldn't let that stand unopposed."

Bernard raised his voice. "Quiet." His voice calmed. "Explosions are homeland security shit. You do know if they find anything other than evidence of a gas leak, they'll go over that scene with a fine-toothed comb. You didn't leave evidence like a mook, did you?"

"Of course not. I made sure we all had masks and gloves," Daniel said, puffing his chest out. "All anyone knows is that some crud filled bar exploded due to the gas line."

"For all our sakes, I hope you're right," Bernard said. "At least this shouldn't blow back on the election. If anything, it may polarize the populace to vote for us. Fear does wonders for persuasion. At least I taught you that much," he stopped in front of Daniel, "even if you are too gung-ho for your own good." He clicked his tongue. "Get out of my sight and lay low." His voice took a steel edge. "I mean it this time, boy. Stay here and out of any hijinks until I call for you."

"I understand."

"Good! Now get out, all of you," Bernard said with a wave of his hand.

The group bowed their heads and, without waiting, exited the double doors.

Bernard tapped his fingers against the cherry wood of the desk. "That'll teach those animals to mess with my little girl. He's still too green for a real squad leadership role, or is he?" Bernard pursed his lips. "Maybe, maybe not," he said to himself.

He grabbed the phone and jabbed at numbers. "One thing's for sure, I'm never short of work."

Tech Room

"It's rare you're down here," Tanya said, yawning. "What's up?"

"You'd know better than I would," Elizabeth said. She sat down beside Tanya. "Rumor was you were involved in my brother's stupid little crusade earlier. I'm honestly surprised you weren't dragged up there to be chewed out."

"I wonder about that," Tanya said, now staring at the monitor in front of her. "I've been here the whole time."

"Uh huh," Elizabeth said with an eyebrow raised. "You're still not a good liar. It was because of the bombing, wasn't it?"

Tanya looked away. "Maybe."

"Oh God, what did they do? Did they start a war?" Elizabeth asked.

Tanya spun her chair around to face her friend. "I think if anyone made the declaration, it was those hood rats."

Elizabeth whistled and showed a toothy grin. "A weak insult, but not entirely wrong. I would have gone with needle dicked losers." She shrugged. "It works. Still, it was asinine to go after them without Daddy's approval. Did he drag Rog along with him?"

"Considering they nearly killed the both of you, I don't think he needed too much convincing. Which reminds me, I need to talk to you about something." Tanya leaned forward. "You two are serious then?"

"What about it?"

Tanya reached up and removed the headphones, placing them beside her on the table. "There are some things you probably should know about him. His si-"

"His sister's sick and needs expensive meds. I know already. We do talk occasionally," Elizabeth said in a smug tone.

"Yes, very good." Tanya's voice dripped with sarcasm. "No doubt you've noticed his other quirks then?"

"What are you talking about?" Elizabeth asked.

"The man cited you as a reason why he went along with your brother. He's impulsive when it comes to those he cares about. That sounds fine and romantic in theory, but have you ever played it out? What if next time he doesn't come back? Your brother rolls up and has the boys drag his carcass out. Do you want to imagine that?"

"What's the point of this?" Elizabeth asked with a scowl. "Fear mongering doesn't suit you."

"I'm saying that you need to reel him in a little. Rog has always been a little wild and impressionable. Your brother isn't exactly the best influence either. You get what I'm saying? Unless you want that, you'd better spell it out to him. He'll do whatever you want. Trust me."

"Why would he?" Elizabeth asked.

"He's the type of guy that gets pussy whipped easily. Make sure your brother knows he'll answer to you if he gets him hurt. That is, if you really want to keep him safe, like he does you."

Elizabeth picked up a stray wire and examined it. "In my experience, men don't generally react favorably to that strategy."

"That's because you've dated prideful meatheads. Rog actually gives a damn about what you think. My bet is he'd do anything to make you happy, like blowing up a building for example. He always did whatever it took to get me to smile when I was down, even when I didn't want him to. It's the kind of guy he is. He avoids confrontation with his friends. Normally I'd never recommend taking advantage of it, but I don't want your brother getting him killed either."

Elizabeth's ruby red lips parted. "You're quite the little strategist, aren't you? You must have been watching and developing that real estate for years. Otherwise, how would you know him so well? You wanted him before I claimed him, huh?"

"This won't be a repeat of prom. Don't worry. You've won this round, as much as I hate to admit it. I won't deny it. I like him. We've been friends for years, but the lunkhead doesn't take hints. You have to strike him over the head with it. That's your territory if there ever was one."

Elizabeth brought a hand to her lips. "Madame, I'm offended. I just don't beat around the bush like some little girls."

"Yeah, whatever," Tanya pouted. "You drop him, and he's fair game again. Deal?"

"That'll be the day. You'd be better served moving on, honey. Maybe join the family by going after Danny?"

"I'd rather puke. That ass never thinks anything through, and it shows in his daily interactions and in his plans. I think he just loves ticking me off." She cracked open a piece of gum and threw it in her mouth.

"I know he does. Still," Elizabeth bit her lip, "I can't let him be dragged along everywhere. It'll catch up to him eventually with how Danny's trying to prove himself to Daddy. I'll go have a talk with him tonight before bed." She stood up and moved to the door but stopped when she heard Tanya's voice.

"Sleeping alone tonight?" Tanya asked, chewing her gum.

Elizabeth turned around. "No, why? Are you jealous? Should I invite you for a threesome? I'm game. I'm sure he'd be up for it."

"Get the hell out before I force you."

They both laughed before Elizabeth stepped outside and closed the door behind her. She walked down the hallway and entered the main lobby. She made her way up the stairs and pushed through the double doors. She saw Daniel, Roger, and Bruce walking alongside each other toward her. She crossed her arms, narrowed her eyes, and tapped her foot on the floor.

"Oh shit." Daniel stopped the group in front of her. "Hi, Sis. How's it going?"

"Leave, Bruce. Now."

"Got it." Bruce slid past her and disappeared behind the doors she'd just entered.

Elizabeth tilted her head. "Rog, go to my room and wait there."

"I just have to go to my room and get something first."

Roger's tone died out toward the end of the sentence under her direct gaze. "Yeah, okay." He trudged forward, his shoulders slumped.

"That was rude. What are you upset about now?" Daniel asked.

"Better rude than stupid like you."

Daniel took a step forward. "You're welcome by the way. They won't try that again."

"Do you want me to swoon and cry 'my hero'?" she asked. "You don't even realize why it was moronic, do you? Let me explain." She poked a finger into his chest. "You had no backup other than Rog and what, Bruce? How many enforcers were there? Answer me that."

"That didn't matter," Daniel said, staring over his sister's shoulder.

Elizabeth stomped her foot. "Of course it matters!" A tear threatened to roll down her cheek as she sniffed. "What would I have done if Rog or, God forbid, you had died?"

"You know the risks of the life, same as me. You'd have dealt with it."

"You're probably right," Elizabeth said. "That doesn't mean it'd have been any easier losing my brother to a selfish revenge romp on my behalf. You've always been selfish, but this takes the cake since you're using me to justify it."

"Believe what you want." Daniel turned his back on her. "It's not like you'll listen once you've got like this anyway."

"Look at me." Elizabeth flipped him around and saw him lock eyes with her. "No more suicide missions. I don't care if it's to save me or not. Do you understand me? For that matter, I'm going with you anytime you drag Rog along."

"Don't trust me with your boy toy?" Daniel sneered.

"One more set of eyes helps on most jobs. With Eddy out

of the loop for the next month or two, you need another person. End of story. It's happening. Deal with it."

"Get off of me." He pushed her off. "You really think dad will let that fly? He'll ground you if he hears word one, especially after that bomb scare."

"Then he'll just have to not hear a single word about it. I trust you'll keep this a secret then?"

"Fine. Things should be settling down."

"Then we're agreed." She reached out a hand.

Daniel grabbed it and shook. "Yeah, fine. Just stay out of our way if it comes to it."

"Sure, sure," Elizabeth said. "Now, if you'll excuse me. I'm going to go and explain to my boyfriend that I'm disappointed in him." She turned and strode away.

"Before you kill him, wait a minute." Daniel reached out.

"What?" Elizabeth asked, looking over her shoulder.

"He did it mostly for you. Take it easy on him, Liz. I need him in good shape."

Elizabeth brought a hand to her mouth and suppressed a giggle. "Dear Brother, are you concerned about your friend or about your career? No matter, he'll enjoy it. Believe that." She faced forward and skipped off behind the door.

"That's what I was afraid of." Daniel sighed, shoved his hands into his pockets, and followed his sister through the door into the lobby.

18

———

"It's been three days. I wonder when our next job will be?" Roger shoved a spoon into the gelatin cup.

"Take it easy, tiger," Elizabeth said beside him on the couch. "It'll happen soon enough. Let's just enjoy the time we have while we can." She snuggled up beside him, earning a round of murmurs around the room.

"You make a good point." His eyes followed a stray woman walking by and drifted lower.

"Obviously," she purred into his side. She reached up, followed his line of sight, and pawed at his arm. "Could you get me a drink, sweetie?"

"Huh?" he asked. He looked back down at her with a warm smile. "Sure. Be right back."

"Take your time," she cooed with a wave. She raised an index finger and gestured toward herself without a word.

Ana came rushing down the stairs. She bent over at the knees, huffing. "Yes, Ms. Morris?"

Elizabeth gestured toward the woman serving the men across the room. "Who's she?"

Ana twisted her head and looked back at Elizabeth.

"Natasha? She's the new girl on the staff. I'm training her as we speak. Did she do something, mistress? Should I have a word with her?"

"No, that's fine. I just wondered is all. Go on, Ana. Don't let me keep you."

Ana bowed. "Yes, madam." She scurried up the stairs, leaving her alone.

"Something wrong?" Roger handed over a can of soda and sat down.

"Nothing. I was just asking Ana something about our newest employee."

Roger took a sip from his can. "You get the answer you wanted?"

"Something like that." She pulled out her phone. "Would you excuse me a second? I have to make a few calls." She placed her drink down on the nearby coffee table and walked into the connecting room.

Bernard's private room...

Bernard rolled over in the luxurious bed with a grunt. A piercing ringing echoed in the quiet room. His arm reached out and clutched the phone. He brought it to his ear. "This better be good."

"Daddy?" Elizabeth asked. "Is this a bad time?"

Bernard sat up, rubbing his eyes with a groan. "What is it?"

"I think you need to send the new girl, Natasha, to go clean up the east wing. I think the boys are using it as a party wing right now."

"Oh, for fuck's sake," Bernard cursed under his breath.

"Fine. Anything else?"

"Nope. Sorry for waking you. I just thought you'd want to know and get ahead of it."

"No problem, dear." Bernard hung up and walked to the door. He ripped it open and barked at the man standing outside. "Get Ana and her new bitch over to the east wing to clean it up. Now!"

"Yes, sir." The man sprinted off down the hallway.

"These kids are going to be the death of me. I just know it." Bernard closed the door and dropped back onto the bed. "They can't even let their old man sleep," he grumbled into his pillow.

In the Lobby...

"Get everything done?" Roger asked.

Elizabeth sat beside him and crossed her leg. "Just had to schedule something. Nothing to talk about."

"Must be hard ordering people around all day," Roger smirked, kicking back in his seat.

Elizabeth leaned forward and flicked Roger's nose. "I'd be careful if I were you, talking to me like that too much," she whispered. "You wouldn't want little old me to get offended, now would you?"

"You have a vicious streak in you," he said.

"Don't you forget it." She grabbed his hand and guided it over her thighs. "Or do I need to remind you how savage I can be?"

"I have an even better idea." Roger sat forward and leaned his forehead against hers. His honeyed voice inching into her ear. "How about we get some privacy, and I can give you one of my private massages?"

"How daring, not to mention lewd. Does any girl actually fall for that line?"

"None of the boring ones. How about it? You don't strike me as boring. You're intriguing, seductive, dangerous, yet I can't stay away. I can't explain it for the life of me," he growled, pulling her closer.

"You do know how to use your tongue, I'll give you that," Elizabeth said. "However, you do have a bad habit of letting your eyes wander. I wonder what I should do about that. I have to keep you entertained," she whispered. "Is that right?" she asked.

"I am a guy. Our eyes wander, but we only grow more ravenous for our own. Does that make sense?"

"It was the most suave attempt at justifying looking at other women that I've ever heard." Elizabeth delivered a peck on his cheek and stood up. "Unfortunately, some of us have work to do today. I'll expect you tonight in my room at midnight sharp. Don't be late." She sashayed off.

19

"The vote's happening as we speak." Eddy changed the channel and placed the remote beside him. "You really think Mr. Alexander has a hope in hell?"

"Don't be stupid." Daniel waved his hand dismissively. "We've drummed up enough fear. The people want to feel safe. After all, they love yelling on television about that crap. You know there's been a few marches now for safer streets led by Alexander. He's getting great PR right before the voting. They eat that up."

"I don't know, brother," Eddy said. "People love their guns. They make them feel safer. I know it works on me. I feel naked without my piece on me. You're the same."

Daniel slapped Eddy's arm. "Normal people aren't like us, goofball. Those sheep are afraid of guns. They're too scared to nut up and face the cold reality that life isn't fair. It's not nice. Sometimes you have no choice but to light a guy up. The world's a cold, ugly, bloody place. They're too scared to admit that so they'll try to get rid of the tool instead, thus perpetuating the problem they're mortified of, crime."

"I think that was the most poetic thing you've ever said in your entire life. That was pretty good. Did you get that from somewhere?" Eddy asked, his mouth quivering until he burst into laughter.

"You dick. I was trying to be deep, and you just veer off into douche land."

"It's in my nature to bust your chops. Nothing personal."

"Anyway," Daniel continued after Eddy's laughter died down, "my point was that I'm not worried."

Eddy muted the television. "Politics isn't an exact science, unless we were physically altering votes. Who knows what all those common folks will vote for. I'd bet the boss has a plan B. He never would go all in on something like this."

"Probably, though he's not told me anything of it. We're getting the Russian guns either way, so even without the scarcity of a ban we'll still make bank. That's where the smart money is, you watch."

"You remind me a lot of your father," Eddy said. "Always trying to see the angles and how you can use them. It brings this old gangster hope for the younger generation." He wiped a fake tear away.

"You're so full of shit." Daniel's snort turned into full blown laughter before clamming up. "Be serious for a minute," he said with a straight face.

"Fine." Eddy cleared his throat. "My prediction isn't a cheery one, brother. A lot of people are talking. There are rumors swirling around that Alexander was involved with your little home visit. It's a massive stain on his campaign. People are worried he's going after his opposition. I'm just saying, don't be surprised if there's an upset tonight."

"Ah, what do you know about politics anyway?" Daniel asked.

"It's just like listening to the pulse of the street. Folks don't like crooks. Doubt is a powerful motivator. Just a hint of doubt at the wrong time can make all the difference. You'd best believe that."

"Want to make a bet?" Daniel pulled out his wallet from his back pocket. "I'll bet a hundred bucks we win tonight."

"I profit either way. Deal," Eddy said. He pulled the pillow out from behind him and fluffed it. "Can't win with an uncomfortable pillow. It wouldn't be polite after all."

"Keep talking. It'll just make my win more satisfying," Daniel said.

The door squeaked open and Bernard entered. He glanced over at the television as he spoke. "We'll know by tonight."

Daniel got up from his chair and allowed his father to take his place. He circled around to the foot of the bed and sat near Eddy's feet. "Probably around midnight, if previous years hold up."

"Which is why I want a hit squad ready to roll up in the middle of the night on Ronald," Bernard said. "Make sure it'll be quiet. No evidence. It'll be a simple in and out. Dispose of the body. Let no one find it. He falls off the face of the earth if he loses. It's as simple as that."

"I'm sorry, boss. What?" Eddy sputtered out.

"It's not good news, my boys. Remember that FBI agent they were sending down to talk to Ronald? If he loses, we cannot allow him to even entertain the thought of talking. If he wins, he's protected."

"How so? What's the difference?" Daniel asked.

"Going after an elected official with a pseudo coup generally dissuades them. The public outcry would echo all the way to Washington. They won't risk losing their funding.

Trust me, they don't give a crap about solving crimes. It always comes back to the almighty dollar."

"Something tells me if they throw that limousine politician into a dark room and ask the hard questions he'd sing like a chorus," Eddy said. "He won't even remember to ask for a lawyer before pissing his pants and blabbing."

"Exactly. We're hedging our bets either way. We'll sell our guns to the highest bidder. The asking price will be higher if he wins, but we'll be alright if not. Always plan for every contingency, and you'll never be caught off guard," Bernard said. He reached over and placed a palm on Eddy's shoulder. "Aside from that, how are you doing, son? Feeling better?"

"I'll be up and at them as soon as they let me, boss."

Bernard chuckled and removed his hand. "I believe that, you tough bastard. It can't come too soon. I need all the professionals I can get around here. For now, focus on getting better. I'll have you working hard when you're up."

"I can't wait to be up and moving around," Eddy said.

"Speaking of which, I'm going to do just that." Bernard pushed himself up and out of his seat and moved to the door. "Take it easy, Edward, and Son, get ready for tonight. Take who you know can get the job done. I'm entrusting you with this. Don't screw it up." He slammed the door behind him as he left.

"Sounds like you just got a job," Eddy said. "Maybe you shouldn't have made that bet. You might have to pay and work. Bet you regret it now."

"Without risk, there is no gain," Daniel said.

Midnight...

"Where the hell is Roger?" Daniel asked the cramped room.

"How would I know?" Bruce asked. He looked back to the door. "I expected him to be here already."

"He's probably in my room, if I had to guess." Elizabeth stole a glance at Bruce. "I told him to be there at midnight, and he didn't want to disappoint me."

"Go get him then." Daniel pointed at the door.

"Okay. I'll be right back." Elizabeth glared at Bruce as she passed him on the way to the door.

"Is she trying to make me jealous?" Bruce asked once Elizabeth had exited the room.

"I think she just likes making you miserable, if I had to guess," Daniel said, standing in front of the podium. "I can't believe we even have to do this, but we're heading over to Alexander's mansion tonight."

"Wait. He lost?" Bruce asked.

"The wonders of living in a goddamned republic are upon us. Apparently people weren't as stupid as we gave them credit for."

"You lost your bet, didn't you? What? You think you're the only one visiting Eddy?" Bruce asked.

"Can we focus on the job at hand, please?" Daniel asked. "We know he has bodyguards all over his property if he's smart. This will leave us with a few options on how to bypass them."

"I can't possibly see how this will be quiet and clean if we're dealing with multiple hostiles before we even get into the damned house," Bruce said. He saw Daniel's narrowed glare. "Just being honest. How the hell do you propose we do this?"

"First, we'd need a little more support than just you and Rog. I've asked Tanya to give us tactical support. She's not here, but she'll give us updates and advice via our phones once we're there. She'll tell us before he leaves his campaign headquarters. We're not going to target him once he's safe and snug inside his house. That's dumb. Instead, we're going to go after his car while he's pulling into his mile-long driveway."

"Explosives?" Bruce asked, shifting in his seat. "That's a dangerous game. Who's going to set that up? I don't know how to handle bombs, and I'm pretty sure you don't either."

"Rog probably does. If he doesn't, we'll simply heft a grenade."

"You're..." Bruce trailed off. "You're joking, right? You must be. None of this is quiet. I expected to climb the fence and hide in the bushes type stuff coming from you. Wouldn't bombs just cause more unwanted attention?"

"Be my guest and scale a ten feet high wall with no training. There's no feasible way that I can see. Even if we did, how would we get out in a hurry, pray tell?" Daniel asked.

"I don't know," Bruce said. "At that point, why not just turn the car into swiss cheese? It'd get the same thing done and be less conspicuous. At least that wouldn't draw the alphabet agencies like sharks to blood."

"That weasel probably has bullet resistant glass and an armored chassis for his limousine."

"You have an answer for everything, don't you?"

Roger's room...

Roger lay on his bed, a white smudge below his nose. He moaned as he twisted on the bed. He heard a knock at the door, along with Elizabeth's stern voice.

"You in there? Didn't you get the memo? We have a job

tonight." Her voice faded for a moment before reasserting itself louder. "I'm coming in."

Loud thuds encompassed the silent room along with the occasional female grunt. "How the hell Danny makes this look simple is beyond me," her voice said through the door. The door eventually shot open, and she shuffled inside. Her eyes grew wide as she moved toward the closed-eyed man. "What in the world?" she asked, looking at his night table. A bag of white powder sat on top. She grabbed it and brought it up. "What is this? Coke? No." She looked down at the unconscious man. She poked him with her free hand. "Are you dead?"

"Mmm." He grunted as he rolled and turned his back to her.

"Look at me, junkie." She pulled his back onto the bed. "Oh, you're out of it. Is this that secret you were so ashamed of? I'm such a great girlfriend I'll even fix this for you. No need to thank me." She carried the bag into the bathroom, dumped the white powder into the toilet, and flushed. "Now to just make sure he makes it through the night." She entered the bedroom and stared at the door. "What do I tell Danny? He can't go in this state." She snapped her fingers. "I've got it."

She pulled out her cell phone and dialed Daniel's number.

"Yeah, where are you? We're going over the plan as we speak," Daniel said.

"New plan. You're not getting me and Rog tonight. We're too busy."

"What?" Daniel barked. "This is no time for your little nookie sprees. We need him here. Now! Do you understand me?"

"It's not possible. I'll explain later, but I'm taking care of him here for the rest of the night. When I'm done with him, he'll never be late again. You can be sure of that. He's about to go through the best rehab program this side of the Mississippi." She flipped the phone shut without waiting for a response. She sat down beside the man and pulled out her handcuffs. She turned him on his side, wrapped one around his hand, and the other around the bed post. She pushed the waste basket close to the bed and stood up. "There. Now you can puke without asphyxiating and still think about what you've done. Be right back, sweetie. I just need to get some things. After you can walk, you're coming to my room."

She closed the door with a thunderous slam, jogging Roger awake. He jerked his hand only to be stopped. One eye forced its way open and saw the steel wrapped around his hand. "Oh no," he slurred.

20

"I can't believe I get to go out on a mission." Tanya bounced in her seat. She looked to the front seat. "Where's Lizzy and Rog though? I thought they were on this as well?"

"They had a change of plans. Trust me, I'll give them a piece of my mind after this," Daniel growled from the passenger seat. "We need to focus on the job. Is the stuff ready?"

"I cobbled it together. It'll blow." She held up a hand-held device, including both buttons and a trigger on the top. All you do is push this button and squeeze this trigger in that order. It'll blow it to smithereens. Now we just need to get it planted. Any volunteers?" She held out the bulky device toward the front.

"I'm not doing it." Bruce leaned away from the explosives.

"The hell you aren't," Daniel said. "You're doing it. Place it right next to the gate, flashing side toward the wall. We don't want them getting wise at the last second."

"You're sure this stuff is stable?" Bruce asked.

"More stable than your mental state," Tanya giggled. "Seriously, you could shoot this stuff and it wouldn't go off. Just trust me," she looked down at the flashing bundle in her hand, "that is, if I wired it correctly. In theory it could go off at any moment. I mean I did have to get these blueprints from some anarchist site. Who knows how reputable that was?"

Bruce extended an open palm and had the device plopped into his grasp. "Be right back." He kept the device steady as he opened the door and exited the vehicle. He ran across the front of the van and to the other side of the street.

"Don't be obvious," Daniel called out as he dashed up to the fence.

"You probably should have done it. He's scared witless. It's not like my joke helped too much," Tanya said.

"No one's around. I'm just busting his balls." He leaned around the seat and eyed her from head to toe. "You've got to have some fun with people, or life's just not worth living."

"That's debatable." Tanya gave a knowing look up front as Bruce scrambled back into the car.

"It's done. Now we just wait?"

"Best get comfy. It'll be a while." Daniel looked at his watch. "It's twelve-thirty now. I bet it'll be three before he finds his way back here. Any preference on music while we wait?"

"Ooh, I love pop." Tanya raised her hand.

"Too bad. We're listening to metal." Daniel turned the radio's dial until a heavy guitar riff roared inside the cabin. He and Bruce head banged as the metal emanated through the cabin.

"Why do I even bother? It's not like he listens." Tanya blew a strand of hair out of her face. She placed a pair of headphones over her ears and placed the laptop at her side onto her lap.

———

Back in detox central...

"Who the hell thought up the idea of a loser giving a speech?" Elizabeth said to the television. "People want to hear from the winner." She kicked the man on the bed in front of her in the side. "Ain't that right?"

"I'm tired. Let me sleep," Roger mumbled into his pillow.

"No. I don't think I will. See, I'm stuck here babysitting your ass when I should be out. If I'm going to be miserable, so will you. This is just beginning, as I'm sure you know. You're still riding high. Come tomorrow, it'll be a whole different ball game. What are those side effects again? I think muscle aches was one of them. Trust me, I'm not going to make that easier on you. We have a lot of exercise planned when you eventually wake up."

"Sorry, could you let me sleep then?" Roger asked, in a rare bout of clarity.

"Sleep?" She jammed her foot into his stomach eliciting a wheeze. "You don't want to sleep today. Come tomorrow you're going to want to sleep through that hell. My job is to make sure you have no energy and can just pass out through the worst of it. You're going cold turkey."

"Seriously?" he gasped.

Her foot found its way lower and hovered, coiled, ready to strike. "I think you should be thanking me. After all, you get my time and attention to dote over your numbed psyche. You should be glad it's not my brother here."

"You told him?" Roger asked, holding his stomach. "He'll kill me."

"No, he won't." She leaned forward and whispered, her voice low and even. "He left that decision up to me." She leaned back and kicked her feet up on the bed. "You're mine. I'm in charge of what goes into your body, since I see you just can't be trusted. You should be honored. I'm molding you into my ideal man." She clasped her hands together. "Every girl wants this chance."

"Every guy dreads it," Roger mumbled under his breath.

"That reminds me." Elizabeth lowered her feet to the ground and reached down beside her chair to the stacked bags. She plucked out a pair of black high heels. She ran a hand over the leopard printed insides. "I think these will look great on me. Shall I try them on now?" She bent over and put on the footwear. She lifted her feet and placed the heels against his chest. "What do you think?"

"Enchanting," Roger's deadpan voice said. "Please have mercy and forgive me already."

She dug the heel around causing Roger to grimace. She leaned forward, exposing a small amount of cleavage. "You sweet fool. This is only the beginning. I won't forgive you so easily."

"Oh, fuck me."

"We'll get to that eventually." She relented and instead placed her legs on top of his body and leaned back. "Do you even know what we're missing right now? You have no idea, do you? You're too off your rocker to hardly know where you are. The world still feels like nothing can go wrong. Is that warm feeling of contentment residing in your belly? You'd better cherish it, because it's the last time you'll ever taste it."

"We're missing something?" Roger tried to sit up only to be shoved back down by her feet.

"You're in no condition to go. You must have overdosed, since I'm guessing you've done this before."

"For a while."

"You're too honest for your own good," Elizabeth said. "What was the original plan? Get hazy and then come over to my room? Let me guess." She raised a finger to her chin. "The drugs help you stay hard longer. Is that right?"

"Think what you like. I'm done explaining myself." His head drooped down. "You don't want to listen anyway."

"I see my leg rest has a bit of fire in its belly. Don't go emo, dear. Your darling is here and will always be." Her sugar sweet voice accentuated the heel digging into his ribs. "Be a good boy. Lie there in silence and learn something."

Roger kept his mouth shut and kept his glazed-over eyes on her.

"Good." She removed her leg and rubbed her hand on his stomach. "You're learning. This will go much easier if you keep that up." She stopped her ministrations and reached over to the night table. "You see this?" She moved a framed picture highlighting a younger Bernard with his children on either side. Elizabeth was hugging her father's leg and standing behind him, while Daniel stood with his chest sticking out.

"Family picture?" Roger asked.

"That's right." She turned it around, her hand trailed down the glass as she spoke. "This was taken right after mom died."

Roger's eyes softened. "I'm sorry. I didn't know."

"Shut up. Obviously you didn't. I just told you." She flipped the photo around and pointed at her younger self. "You see this? Tell me what you see."

Roger squinted at the picture. He looked back up at her.

"A scared little girl, afraid of losing her daddy and those she loves."

"You have an annoying way of wording things." She placed the frame back on the nightstand and frowned. "You're not wrong."

"I'm sorry for scaring you."

She pursed her lips and stared at the news reel passing by on the screen. "You should be. You're just lucky I'm such a nice person, giving you another chance like this."

Roger's hand jerked against the metal cuffs causing a clinking sound. "You need to undo these for a minute."

"Now, why would little old me do that?" Elizabeth asked. "What incentive do I have?"

"I need to go."

"Go?" Elizabeth asked, looking toward the door. "Go where?"

A low growl came from Roger's throat until he saw Elizabeth holding in a laugh.

"Don't worry. I'm not dealing with that. Here." She dug in her pocket, retrieved the key, and leaned over to unlock the cuffs. "Go. Enjoy this because it's the only time I'm taking them off."

Roger sat up, holding his head. "Fantastic." He stood up on wobbly feet and took slow steps across the room. "I'll be right back."

"I have to make a call anyway." She pulled out her phone and tapped the screen multiple times. She lifted the phone to her ear.

21

"Hopefully Liz remembered to watch like I told her to," Tanya said. She puffed her cheeks out. "This is so boring. How do you people do this so often?"

"Necessity. Same way you do your tech wizard stuff," Daniel said. "Welcome to the ugly side of the job."

"If you're not careful, you'll get a dvt doing this too often." She extended her legs and lifted her arms behind her head with a yawn. "At least I have my laptop. You two just keep staring at that unmoving cityscape." She reached for her laptop until a vibration in her pocket interrupted her. She whipped out her phone and looked at the text. "Scratch that. He left the convention center about ten minutes ago. He should be here any time. Get ready with that detonator."

Daniel flipped open the cover on the trigger and held it at the ready. "Already ahead of you." He stared at the mirror outside his window. "I'll be ready."

"I have his GPS coordinates. It looks like he'll be here inside of two minutes."

"How do you know his phone number?" Daniel asked, not looking away from the mirror.

"When you act as the go between for the boss, you come across this kind of information. He just pulled onto the street beside ours. Get ready. They'll be here inside of a minute." She ducked down behind the seats. "I'd recommend Brucie follow suit. We don't want to spook them by showing ourselves.

"Fine," Bruce grumbled, lowering his head.

Daniel slid down his seat until he could barely see out the window. "It's showtime, ladies and gentlemen," he said in a soft voice.

A pair of headlights shone inside the windows and grew more intense as the limousine came closer. It slowed down as it approached the fenced off gate and turned. It sat in front of the gate as a hand reached out of the driver's side to push the intercom.

"Gotcha," Daniel said with a squeeze of the cherry red button on the top. He squeezed the trigger, causing a flash of light and the sound of shattering glass to echo across the block. The car rolled over and slammed into the opposite wall and settled upside down. A nearby parked car's alarm rang incessantly.

"He's gone," Daniel said. He reached over and nudged Bruce's shoulder. "Go."

"Wait a minute." Tanya pressed her face against the glass. "Someone's getting out."

"You're joking." Daniel analyzed the wreckage to see that a man was indeed crawling out of the back seat, bloody.

He clawed his way out of the twisted metal and over the leaked gasoline to the relative safety of the sidewalk.

"Be right back." Daniel threw the car door open and marched over to the surviving person. He squatted down and grabbed the man's hand, dragging him across the pavement toward the back of the van.

"Oh no. He's not thinking about -" Tanya climbed over the seats once Daniel disappeared behind the van. "Yes, he is." She threw the back doors open."

Daniel hefted the squirming man into the back, face down. He shut the doors in Tanya's face.

He circled around the car and climbed in. "Go."

The car jerked forward as Tanya placed her hand on the side of the cabin. "What am I supposed to do with this? He's charred all over." She laid a dainty finger on the side of his neck. "He's still alive somehow, lucky bunny."

"There's duct tape there," Daniel said with a flick of his wrist. "Use it to restrain him so he doesn't cause any mischief. We'll be escorting him to his final resting place before you know it."

"I never signed up for this," Tanya said under her breath. She reached over to the sliding roll of tape and tore off a piece. She dragged his hands behind him with a squeak of exertion and binded him. "Where are we going?"

"Someplace no one will ever find his rotting carcass."

"Bay or forest?" Bruce asked, stepping on the brake.

"We have no cinder blocks, so we're taking a hike tonight."

"Roger that." Bruce flicked the turn signal and pushed the gas. "It'll be a long night, but at least we'll be done."

"For now," Daniel said. He peeked around the back of his seat to see Tanya struggling to tie him up. He climbed over the seats and sat beside her. "Let me help."

"Finally." Tanya's palms fell to her sides and laid flat on the floor as she reclined back. She looked to her left. "That's what the shovels are for, eh? Dirty, but effective."

"Welcome to my life," Daniel said with a yank of

Ronald's ankle. "There." He slapped Ronald's unmoving body. "You're all set now." He looked up at Tanya. "Good job, I guess."

"That's rare," Tanya said. "If you're not careful, someone might think you actually have emotions."

"Can't have that," Bruce chimed in from the front.

"Quiet up there," Daniel barked. He scooted next to Tanya and leaned over to whisper in her ear. "I know this isn't what you're used to. I just wanted to let you know I appreciate it. That's all." He returned to the front seat, leaving a flustered, red faced Tanya staring at the floor.

"Dummy," Tanya murmured.

An hour later...

"We're here finally." Bruce twisted the key and removed it. "Time to finish work. You may want to stay in here, sweet thing." He gave a shit eating grin into the rear-view mirror.

"As if you have a chance, butthole." Tanya crossed her arms and pouted. She reached over and swiped the touch pad on her laptop. "Aw, poo. The battery's almost dead."

A thump in the back caused her to jump. She got on her knees, turned around, and peeked over the seat. "Awake?"

"Mmm," Ronald said through the gag. He kicked his legs and flopped around.

"Yeah, I have no idea what you're saying," Tanya said. "I have good news and bad news. The good news is you won't suffer for long - I think. You want to hear the bad?"

He shook his head.

"I wouldn't either."

The back doors flung open.

Tanya pointed at the two men. "They're your bad news."

Bruce reached into the cabin and clutched Ronald's ankle. "That's right. You are ours now." He looked over at Daniel. "I need some target practice. How about you?"

Daniel pulled out his pistol and examined it. "Yeah, I could use some. Let's go set up the target, shall we?"

"You'll need this." Tanya tossed the roll of tape to Bruce. He tucked it inside his coat pocket and reached in.

Ronald's eyes widened and he tried to slide away from the encroaching limbs. He kicked both legs up in the air and slammed down onto Bruce's hand.

"Son of a bitch." Bruce waved his hand and sucked on his thumb. "He got my thumb with that foot. Be careful, bro."

"Just for that, it won't be quick." Daniel dragged Ronald close to the edge by his foot. "Watch your step, asshole." He pulled hard with a grunt, causing Ronald to slam hard onto the dusty ground. "The first step's always a doozy." He looked to Bruce. "I wonder if it's the same in politics."

"Don't know." He stopped fanning his hand and reached down. "He's about to learn how it works in the real world. Assault someone, and we don't call for committee investigations. We take care of it ourselves." He reached down, grabbed the other foot, and started dragging him away.

They closed the door and dragged him deeper into the surrounding tree line, leaving Tanya by herself.

"Do I even want to watch that?" She looked at her blinking laptop and back to the window. "I think I'd rather call Lizzie." She pulled out her phone and dialed.

Deeper in the brush...

"This could have all been avoided, Mr. Alexander," Daniel said as they dragged him through a bush by the legs. "All you had to do was win. I have a personal stake in this, you see. You let me down. I guess that's what I get for not voting."

"He lost a bet that you'd win. He owes a hundred bucks," Bruce said with a laugh.

"Yes. You've cost not just me but our entire organization money and safety. See, we can't allow this whole investigation business to play out. We're doing you a favor really, when you look at it. Ain't that right, Bruce?"

"Yeah, you wouldn't survive two days inside once you squealed. It's best to just tie up loose ends preemptive like. It's just the rules of the game. You knew it when you entered. If you didn't, congratulations. You're stupid."

Daniel pointed toward a large tree just ahead. "That looks like a good spot. They dragged him and stood him up against it. "I'll hold him while you tape."

"You got it." Bruce started at Ronald's chest and circled around the tree, using more tape with every pass. "This seems like such a waste of tape," he remarked as he passed Daniel and lifted the tape above.

"There's no price on fun. You need to remember that," Daniel said, holding the struggling man.

"That should do it." Bruce tore off the colossal piece of tape. "You want first crack, since he cost you the most?"

Daniel whipped out his pistol and pulled back the slide with a click. "Sure." They backed up ten paces. Daniel aimed center mass and squeezed the trigger.

A muffled howl was heard, and a spreading red stain appeared on Ronald's stomach.

They walked up and inspected the gaping hole. "Gut shots are always the worst I hear," Daniel said, poking a finger with a squelch into the wound. He flicked the bile off his hand and looked at Bruce. "Your turn."

"With pleasure." They backed up again, this time Bruce aiming his 9mm. "Where shall I aim? Any preferences?" His aim fell to Ronald's groin. "As thanks for the bruised thumb, I thought he might not need his dick anymore. What do you think?"

Daniel reached over and moved his aim a few inches up. "Nah, man. He'd die too quick. Shoot it through his pelvis. It's even more painful and not quite as fatal. I mean, there are still arteries there. But if you took his dick off, he'd die inside two minutes."

"Huh," Bruce said, "today I learned something new." He squeezed the trigger and another muffled cry rang out. "Ooh," he said walking forward, "now that has to hurt. Does it hurt worse than when you try to pee and stop halfway through?" He waited for a response only to find silence. "I'll just assume you said worse." He got in his face and spat as he spoke. "You'd already be dead if you hadn't smashed my thumb. Was it worth it?"

"Alright," Daniel rested a hand on Bruce and pulled him away, "let's end this. We've had our fun." Daniel unsheathed his knife and cut apart the silver tape.

Ronald tumbled to the ground, writhing in agony. He fell onto his stomach, looked up, and saw the full moon behind the two men.

Daniel raised his weapon and leveled it at Ronald's head. "This is where your story ends." His finger squeezed the trigger. A shot rang out, causing a flock of birds to emerge from the trees.

22

"It's done then?" Bernard asked, sticking a stogie into his mouth and puffing on it. "Good job, Son. Come on home after you dispose of the trash, and we'll figure out our next move." He hung up, slamming down the receiver. He looked up at Elizabeth standing in front of his desk. "Your brother's done. What is it?"

"I'm going with him and Rog from now on, and you can't stop me."

"It's not happening. You only have a rudimentary knowledge of firearms. You'd be more of a liability than an asset, dear."

"You don't understand." Elizabeth's hands fell to her hips. "This isn't a question."

Bernard stood up. "Are you trying to tell me you're disobeying my orders?"

"I need to know how to run this place. What better way to do that than to follow your successor and his wonder boy around? Danny would never let anything happen to me, especially with Rog there beside me."

"No, it's out of the question." Bernard lowered himself

back into his seat. "You're my little girl, and you're not going out there until you're ready."

"I'm not giving you a choice, old man. Do you really think you can keep me in here against my will? You'll have some unconscious guards soon enough."

Bernard massaged his temples. "Why do you have to make everything difficult, honey?" He dug through the drawers. "He's not ready to keep you safe yet. That kid can barely keep his own hide in one piece, much less anyone else."

"Roger has kept all of us alive, including you. Remember?"

Bernard shoved the drawer shut and threw a black notebook on the desk. "Yes, you do have a point. You really want him to be responsible for your safety? Remember, he went along with your brother and that yahoo in a revenge rampage."

Elizabeth held her hands behind her back and fidgeted. "I've let him know why he won't be doing that again."

Bernard scoffed. "I believe that." He sighed. "Fine. You be careful. And have him take you to the field to practice with your .44. You may need to use it, and you can't always depend on someone else. Do that, wear kevlar, and I'll say yes."

"Deal." Elizabeth jumped up and clapped. She put on her sweetest voice. "Thank you, Daddy."

"Just let me work."

"Okay." Elizabeth bounced as she turned around and made for the door.

"You're going to wear that vest every single time you go out, young lady. Every single time. I don't care if it's to the store or on a job. Do you hear me?"

"Always," she answered, not bothering to turn around. "Don't worry about me," she said, reaching the door.

"That's just something I can't do." Bernard reached for the notebook and opened it.

"Night, Dad." She closed the door and was skipping down the hallway when her phone rang. "Hello?"

"Everything going alright back there?" Tanya asked.

Elizabeth walked down the hallway past a maid. "Better than I could have hoped for. Rog isn't feeling well right now, but I'm nursing him back to health. Are you bored or something? Why are you calling?"

"About that..." Tanya trailed off. "Your brother and his friend are out. I decided to call you. Is that so wrong for a friend to do?"

Elizabeth slid the red tapestry to the side of the nearest window and stood before it, gazing outside. "It doesn't sound like you, unless the battery on that laptop is low. That's it, isn't it?"

"Partially, but I'm a little nervous, given the circumstances."

"I can only imagine," Elizabeth said. "Just take a deep breath. Panicking won't help anything."

"Is Rog alright? He's not here," Tanya said. "I have to assume no?"

"I told you, he's fine but indisposed."

Tanya sniffed. "It was the H again, wasn't it? Did you think I didn't know? Whenever he used to bail on appointments, I'd usually find out he'd been locked up in his room away from his sister. I'd just impersonate his girlfriend. They let me right in. He spilled the beans when I called him out on it. As his best friend, I appreciate you trying to keep his image intact like a good girlfriend. He didn't OD did he?"

"He's in my rehab. You can rest assured he'll be fine. Possibly a little sore, but he'll have no lasting damage."

Tanya choked back a sob, and in a shaky voice said. "I know he's in good hands then. Just don't be too rough. He'll be jonesing hard in a couple days. He'll be in enough pain without you kicking him or whatever it is that gets you off."

"I'll be the judge of that. You just focus on aiming for my bonehead brother's heart if you want a shot at happiness."

"You always were a bitch," Tanya said.

"Like you've changed much."

In the forest...

"This guy's heavier than he looks," Bruce said.

"It's fine, weakling." Daniel lifted Ronald's other shoulder higher. "You just need to lift more and stop eating so many chips. That's all that is." He looked down at Bruce's legs. "Are you lifting with your legs or your potbelly and back?"

Bruce's hand fell to his gut. "The last time we were at the gym I remember different results at the bench press."

"That's because the last time we went was over a year ago, chubby," Daniel said as they approached the makeshift grave. "Ready?"

"As ever."

The men dumped the limp body into the hole.

"No one should ever find him this far out in the state park, should they?" Bruce asked, grabbing the shovel sticking out of the mound of nearby dirt.

Daniel jarred the other loose and filled in the hole. "Not

if we do our jobs right. It's well off the hikers' paths, six feet deep, and not near any campsites that I know of."

"You mind if I ask you something?" Bruce said, shoveling another load of dirt into the grave.

"You're going to anyway, so get it over with."

"You've got a thing for that girl in there. I can tell by the way you look at her."

Daniel rolled his eyes and heaved another shovelful. "That's not a question, dumbass."

"Tell me you're going after it. You two would be perfect together. They say opposites attract. Why not give it a shot?"

"Because not all of us guys are looking to get our dick wet all the time. Some of us prefer to prioritize our career first. The love will come later."

"I don't buy it."

"Fine," Daniel said. "You asked, I answered. Are we done?"

Bruce spiked the shovel into the soil and leaned on it. "Yeah, no need to be so short."

"We're doing the equivalent of digging a ditch twice in a short period of time, and you wonder why I'm annoyed by inane conversation?" Daniel asked, wiping his brow. "Fine, I want to be home right now flirting with that cute blonde girl." He held the shovel as he swung it at empty air in front of Bruce. "Is that the answer you wanted to hear?"

"I was just saying, bro."

23

———

"Where is he?" Daniel side stepped, only to have his sister match him.

"He's under my protection," Elizabeth said. "You're not touching him."

"What the hell happened?" Daniel cracked his knuckles. "Why didn't he show up last night?" Daniel asked in a shushed voice.

Elizabeth took her brother's arm and guided him into a nearby empty bedroom. She closed the door behind them. "He couldn't even get up. He had a habit he never told anyone besides Tanya about. If you want to know more, ask her. I'll not tell. I will say he'll never do it again. You have my word on that."

"You're taking responsibility for him?" Daniel sat down on the vacant bed and kept his gaze on the carpet. "I never thought I'd see the day." He was quiet for a few seconds before he lifted his head. "When will he be up and around again? I assume it'll be a while with your methods."

"Give me a week, and he'll be better than new."

"It must have been bad if you need a week."

Elizabeth sat next to her brother. "It was heroin, Danny. He was off his ass when the order came down last night. I had to make sure he didn't choke on his own vomit. It wasn't exactly glamorous. The only reason I'm telling you is because I know you can keep it quiet."

"Motherfucker." Daniel punched down into the bed. "This never gets out. No one can know about this."

"Otherwise you look bad. I know how the game's played."

"I need to talk to him before you finish your little indoctrination."

"How rude." Elizabeth brought a hand up to her ample chest. "I'm simply doing this for everyone's own good."

"I bet," Daniel said. "My statement still stands. I will say my piece before the end of the day. Agreed?"

"It's not like I have a choice. There's one more piece of news for today you should know of."

"What's that?"

"I got Dad's permission to join your merry little group. Mainly to oversee my ongoing commitment to Rog's willpower." She smirked. "A girl needs to oversee her investment after all."

"Normally you just throw them away, not work on them," Daniel said. "He must have made an impression on you. Regardless," he stood up, "I'm going to go see him now before your hell week or whatever it is you have planned. You want my advice? Show no mercy. At the end of the week he'll never want to touch the stuff. Don't coddle him." He walked to the door and stopped after he opened it. "I take it he's in your room?" he asked.

"Yeah, don't take too long. My schedule is full of his reeducation."

"I'd never dream of it." Daniel closed the door behind

him and began the trek to his sister's room. "I can't believe it. How did I not see it?" He pushed open the nearby door and passed through it. "There he is." He took a step forward. "Not feeling well, sunshine?" His nose crinkled after he looked down at the waste basket. "Puking I see." He pinched his nose. "Jesus, dude. What the hell were you thinking?"

"I wasn't. In fact, that was the Goddamned point," Roger moaned.

"Isn't that what all junkies say? I can't believe you fooled me. It's rare to find a functioning H junkie. I thought you were unicorns or something, so I didn't even entertain the idea. I see now that was a mistake."

"This life is dirty and ugly. I don't see how you people do it without help."

Daniel lunged forward with a punch to Roger's exposed stomach. "You deal with it and face it head on. You don't run away from life like a coward, you little shit. The only reason you're not being crucified for this is my sister. I wouldn't thank her yet. I told her to go hard on you. You need to learn how to deal with this life, one way or the other. You will by the time she's done with you. If not, I get my turn. Do you understand me?" He grabbed a hand full of hair and lifted Roger's head by his hair. "I didn't hear an answer."

"I got it," Roger wheezed out. "I'm sorry."

"That may drench my sister's panties, but that doesn't work with me. Actions speak louder than words. You're going to have to earn back my trust like a man, not a pussy."

Roger rolled onto his back. "I'll do whatever it takes."

"That's a good start. See to it that you finish it. I'll be getting daily status reports from her. Do not disappoint me." He stomped out of the room to find Elizabeth standing outside, leaning against the opposite wall.

"Finished? That was tame for you."

Daniel shut the door. "Sometimes the carrot works better than the stick."

"That was the carrot?" Elizabeth asked. "Looked like the stick plus a dose of blackmail."

Daniel ran a hand through his hair with a deep inhale. "Believe me, you'd know if I used the stick. He'd have to be carried out. A little tap to his breadbasket is mild compared to what I wanted to do last night." He strode off toward the lobby. "Have fun, Sis."

"You know it." Elizabeth turned her attention back to the door. "I always do."

***

Recovery Ward later that day...

"I wish I'd been there last night," Eddy said.

Daniel leaned against the railings of the bed. "You and me both." He stared blankly past Eddy.

"What's wrong, brother?" Eddy asked. "Don't say nothing. I can tell. What happened?"

"Roger let me down last night in a big way. We're lucky everything didn't go to hell because of his choices."

"The kid's under a lot of pressure, Danny. He may be tasked with keeping you safe, but you need to look out after him too. That's what brotherhood is. Look, I'm not saying cuddle with him, but an honest exchange can solve a lot of problems."

"We had one earlier. I don't think he'll forget it either. It's moot anyway. Elizabeth's retraining him in her room for the next week. I have faith he'll be fit for duty after that."

"That," Eddy said, "or he'll need a psychiatrist from all the damage." The two men shared a laugh. "I have faith in the kid. Your sister's motivations, not as much. It looks kind of unhealthy to me."

"What's unhealthy is if my father found out why last night happened."

"You never did tell me why."

"No, I didn't," Daniel said. "There must be a reason for that."

"Covering for him?" Eddy asked. "I guess you do like him well enough. He's in good hands. I won't ask further, but just look out for him, huh? For me."

"Alright, you sap. Fine. I'll do it," he stole a glance down at the man, "if you really want me to."

"You're going to get soft at this rate."

Daniel reached down and pinched his ear. "Shut your mouth when the situation calls for it, you idiot."

"I love this family."

24

"How are you feeling, you jerk?" Daniel slapped Roger's back. "You better be ready to head back to work. Fun time is over."

"You call that fun?" Roger's voice picked up a few octaves. "That made the army ranger's hell week look like a vacation to Hawaii. Do you know what she did? Of course you do. You got updates daily. You probably gave her some of those ideas, didn't you? Don't lie."

Daniel held his hands up in a surrendering gesture. "I lied. I was in the dark the whole week. I just said that to scare you." He punched Roger's shoulder. "Did it work?"

"Fricking right it did."

"Then good. You're welcome. Come on." He pointed ahead. "Dad wants to see us." The two walked side by side.

"You didn't tell anyone else?" Roger asked.

"Are you stupid? No, I'm on the hook for you for better or worse."

The two turned the corner and saw a man at the end of the hall in front of the telltale double doors. "I didn't tell the boss either. Just keep your mouth shut," Daniel said out of the side of his mouth.

They stopped in front of the sunglasses clad man. "Here to see the boss," Daniel announced.

"Go right in, Mr. Morris." He opened the door and shut it behind them.

"About time you got here." Bernard heaved his feet on top of the desk and reclined. "It's been a whole week, and I have just one thing to say. Do you consider explosives quiet? I don't. I remember saying be quiet with the hit. It worked out all the same, but you fucked up. While we didn't get everything we wanted, we're still whole. You can't take that for granted. It's mostly due to you two." Bernard dug into his coat pocket and fished out a single bullet. He tossed it underhanded to his son. "You know what that is?"

Daniel caught it and brought it up to his face. He twisted and inspected it. "9mm. What about it?"

"That is the bullet my pappy gave me when I was ready. You know what that means? It's official. Go ahead and pick your team. I'd recommend keeping it small, but I need Eddy to head his own group."

"I'll get right on it, Pop." Daniel pumped his fist with a wide grin. "Leave it to me."

"You two are dismissed. Go to work, you lazy bums. I have work to do."

"Yes, sir," both men answered in unison.

The next morning.

"You're not picking anyone else?" Elizabeth asked. "We can't function with just three people. We need at least one more."

"Fine." Daniel disassembled his gun and began the laborious process of cleaning it. "I hear there's a new guy joining up today. I'll go have a look at him when I'm done. Happy?"

"I heard he's had army training. He should be able to keep you in line, or at least alive if nothing else," Elizabeth said.

"Army grunts know how to do what they're told," Daniel said. "The only problem is some of them have that annoying sense of righteousness to them. I don't need that."

"Then I assume you'll teach him to keep his mouth shut. You're his boss, if you take him."

"At least he knows how to kill and get the job done. Unlike that ex-boyfriend of yours. All he does is bitch and moan on the job." Daniel tossed the bore brush onto the table and reassembled the firearm. He aimed down the sites and cocked it. "I'll test him tonight if that'll make you happy."

"Awesome. Now let's go celebrate with a trip to the range." Elizabeth unholstered her .44 and walked toward the front door.

"Fine." Daniel shoved the pistol down the front of his jeans and cupped a hand to his mouth. "Rog, get over here. We're going to improve your terrible aiming today."

"It's not that bad, come on." Roger sidled over. "That new guy's pretty tough," he said with a thumb jabbed over his shoulder. "Have you heard his war stories yet?"

Elizabeth latched onto his arm and laid her head to rest in the crook of his neck. "Not yet."

Daniel stood up and led the group toward the front door. "Stories can always be exaggerated. What truly matters is how you deal with bad situations on the fly. Anyone can be daring when recalling, few can when it truly matters. Now let's go prepare to take over our city." They pushed the door open and stepped into the sunlight.

The End

THANK YOU FOR READING!

The adventures of the Morris family continue in The Silver Lining, already out now. If you'd like to support this work, please consider leaving a rating or review on Amazon. Have a great day!

ABOUT THE AUTHOR

Alex J Fischer has been writing for close to a decade and has won six National Novel Writing Month challenges in a row.

Alex grew up in a small town in Ohio and still resides there. Hobbies include writing, video games, and watching crime shows.

ALSO BY ALEX J. FISCHER

The Morris Crime Family:

Welcome to the Family

The Silver Lining

Any Means Necessary

The Fourth Bullet

A New Generation

Full Circle

Order of Vengeance Motorcycle Club:

The Order of Vengeance

Vengeance Above All

Masked Justice:

The End of Innocence

Masked Justice

Blind Justice

The Collector:

The Debt Collector